STORY OF A GIRL

Withdrawn from Stock

For Ger

STORY OF A GIRL

Tom Mac Intyre

LILLIPUT PRESS
DUBLIN

First published 2003 by
THE LILLIPUT PRESS LTD
62–63 Sitric Road, Arbour Hill,
Dublin 7, Ireland
www.lilliputpress.ie

A CIP record for this title is available
from The British Library.

1 3 5 7 9 10 8 6 4 2

ISBN 1 84351 014 6

The Lilliput Press receives financial assistance from
An Chomhairle Ealaíon / The Arts Council of Ireland.

Set in 10 on 14 Palatino and Optima
Printed in Ireland by ßetaprint of Dublin

STORY OF A GIRL

Soil is not stone on stone

The Only Girl

A girl sat on the swing which hung from the lowest branch of a fir stationed between paired beeches. Her hands, too firmly, clutched the ropes of the swing. No arrived look in the eyes. She had, quick after a fashion, gathered ways of behaviour to disguise this something lacking but such devices of the imitative could only serve so far, the imitative so naked, the echo definably echo, at speed the passing stranger knew. One reckoning glance. Some lack in her eyes. And the only girl. Such a shame.

A litany of possible roads. Pray. Offer it up. Have masses read. Sigh in the candled dusk of Bridget's February pattern. Go on larger pilgrimage. Write to healers, there was one in Carlow. Laying on of hands (generally). Look down. Look up. Smile and like it. Caress her hair. Hold her. Make her the centre of the room. Make her the way to the room, the way out. Think of lessons she might take. Knit for her, cardigans, foot-warmers, gloves. Have her photographed every birthday (18 January). Allow her to play – within bounds. She had a tendency to roam, the town, the shops, back rooms of old women on the prowl for pastime. Laugh with her. She could too, laugh. She had her own genuine albeit restricted laughter, from what well was hard to say.

How had this come? And what to be done? Two questions, spawning questions, all rolled to one question. The question could be listened to but not discussed. It was easier, in a way, if you listened, if there was agreement on that, and, more or less, there was. A provisional agreement that certain matters were best left to the lick of circumstance, next year, the year after. This had its own burdens but it was a resolution (or the scaffolding of such) provided some stay. Further, that agreed approach was permitted, and this was healthy, to contradict itself intermittently. Burdened question, that is to say, might be discussed – but not listened to. These tough flavours of resource. As the girl sits on the swing and crows debate a thinning of the light.

The word *fontanelle*. The word *fontanelle* flew like a bird about the lawn and between the trees. A songless bird. If it could be made to sing, to serenade, the done might be undone, but *fontanelle*, in the end of the day, was not that docile. A careless maid, said the holly, before the *fontanelle* was closed, left the child too long in an unruly sun. The sun poured through a gap and left its print. That could not, it seemed, now be removed, it was too far in, lodged. *Fontanelle*. The membrane. The curtain. The door. But no one believed a word of that story. There was no story. All was fiction. Except that absence in the eyes.

Shadow discerned, stare of the shadow inescapable, the expert was consulted. Saunders was the best in Ireland. There was the man who would not speculate, who could say what was, look in the window and ponder and articulate his preferred reading concerning the beautiful, the wilting, three she would have been, there or thereabouts. Saunders spoke. 'She'll be fine.' Lag of some kind, he'd go so far as, a disinclination to hurry, it was perfectly normal, the child would be fine. Without the slightest difficulty, making figures on the white wall of the consulting-room with his long educated fingers, he summoned her laugh. And packed them all off home. Thinking of that laughter, improbable rakish furligig. There was the bother, the nut to digest, comprehend. Acknowledge, yes, an absence in the eyes (although Saunders would not have gone with that) but when it pleased her, or pleased the fancies in her head, or those in charge of those fancies, she had a laughter, ripple and rebus, entirely her.

'Saunders said she'd be fine.' Sentence that entered the weather of the grounds, blended with rising and descending sap,

8

rambling tints of the grass, snowdrop, daffodil, lilac yet to be; at its royal ease, that sentence become verdict moved into the house, took over furniture, utensils, reflections, door-sounds, slop-sounds, wind in the furred chimneys, jandied black of the blazing newspaper set against an upright tongs in hope to induce draught, excite a dull fire; no crevice or wrinkle of clock or calendar but harboured, nourished, and proprietorially distributed the mantra – *Saunders said she'd be fine.*

The soil exceptionally sticky, water has difficulty finding a way. Getting a lift presented comparable problems. Near Dulane, an old man, wheezing incantations, put a needle to your corpulent knee. You drop, felled ox. When you rise, she's lying on the ground, herself, breastplates – your focus – silver beneath her hands.

And grey, in dun light, there's a bird with young (one) on shoulder, a wall by them, opposite this pair a bat, half-effigy, half-alive.

4 September

Meeting with JJ in Switzerland, country house, simple unpretentious, in a rolling meadow, and that, out of all the stories, slope to a stream. I'm found to be sitting outside, and here he comes, without appointment, always, dapper mischiefy fierce soul-shining, smiling, looking into me warmly, he's still approaching, I'm still seated, now, have we met? Everything alters, he's seated, the normal conversational distance away, I'm trained on him – FLIP – and he's floaty above his chair, at once a drawing and human, an oscillation, bird-man, spilling alpha beta gammas Cyrillic Greek Ogham English fibrelations, Fecund Be Thy Name, who is looking into my life with candour and love and submarine might. I look back, aware I'm being plumbed, and this lasts, is momentary, never was. Later, in the house with a woman – Norah? – she's hospitable, wise. *Fáilte*, Hyacinth. View of meadow through the window, through a door JJ visible in the garden, mere ten yards away. I want to be with him but there are obligations, courtesies. (I'm aware he's keeping an eye.) She's enquiring, well she might, about the company I keep back on the Liffey's ardent swell. Names? A name? A difficulty remembering – seems so long ago, such a distance. Kerns, I come up with. Accepted, she'll settle for that. Rough rug-headed, to the last man. Food for powder. Commander-in-Chief: Furor Celticus. Deputy Commander: *Fág an bealach!* Never more dangerous than when in full retreat.

Queen to Behold

'Correct!'

Plenitude of iron in that parish, iron well-wrought the gates of The Villa, front and back. Opened in a southerly wind, the front gate cried, a wail flew, entered the living-room, bounced off the fly-blown sideboard mirror, fell disconsolately at our feet. This must be the hounded evening intruder. Go out to the porch and check; front window – curtains, shutters, blind – a day's work, and giveaway. There, bicycle-lamp dull on the avenue, he was pushing the bike along under the pissing trees, no hurry, and he had occupation. Long idle, he had, of late, occupation, it lent him scope undreamt of, planed his jaw-line, steadied the cut of his hams as he sat poised to knead beatitudes.

The kitchen. Across the gravel, around the house, into the back yard. Of the people, he would not condone the front door, no, let it be the yard, snug rectangle of outbuildings partially lit, stronghold warmth of the kitchen. The offered chair he settled mid-stage – this was *his* performance, spectators might circle *him*, nicely arranged, lit a cigarette, and waited for the cup of tea. It arrived. He tasted, starved lips nursing the rim, so many cups, hard to learn them all, never mind tame them. First slug. Grand. The cap on his head, minute shift. And, signature tic, return to previous inclination. Speak. 'She's a grand wee woman. One of the best! She's a flamer, fifteen-carat gold and the light in her eye, I'll warrant ye! Now, give it to me straight and give it to me true, is she, or is she not, a flamer? What? Correct!' 'Correct!'

The word *correct* had never been sounded like this, hadn't been broached till now. It had been waiting for Jemmy Cullen to take, fix in his sights, pierce in triumph and in triumph tap its innermost mathematical sureties – '*Correct!*' – no one who heard Jemmy free that word would ever forget the sound, it combined disbelief (that he should be so lucky), obstinacy, comfortably pressing griefs – would he, would anyone, ever be able to meet the demands carousing in this rabid flow, the timbre hugged ecstasy, every excess of the lunatic, tossed straitjacket, lifejacket, compass, to the four reeling and lesser quarters, submerged in bright fathoms coursing the hour, surfaced as crown on drenched Jemmy who laughed and looked at those he'd left behind, crusted in the ordinary, and cried and cried again – '*Correct!*'

The flagged floor looked up at him. He smiled for it, played with the cigarette, rolled the tea around in his cup. Motion of the tea in that cup beguiled. He winked for it, gurgled, chuckled, moaned, informed his horse, best in the townland, that the horse must go – 'Yer a quality bayste but – no sin on *your* back – ye'll have to go.' Farm machinery also, land if necessary, every last rood, the bother was he must have a motor-car for these night journeys. 'A body needs comfort on the road. Man or woman, woman or man, who'd be looking for hardship? Isn't that right, gossoon?' The boy nodded. 'Isn't that a fact, *gearcaile*?' The girl's eyes opened wider than usual. 'What's your name?' she asked the question she always asked – she wanted, again, to hear him evade the question. 'Butter-an'-crame,' Jemmy Cullen obliged. 'Matter a damn, the horse – *will be will be* – has to go.'

The cat, a calico Tom, rose from near the Stanley, paraded the flags, viewed this demanding intruder, returned to the heat. 'I want a horse,' the girl said. 'Give me the horse.' Jemmy focussed on a point a little to the left of the girl. 'I do watch her serving drinks behind that counter,' said Jemmy. 'A queen to behold. On the pinnacle o' time. And she knows, they know, they have eggs that know, the lie o' the hill. I said to meself – had to be said – I said to meself, *Mary, this horse has to go.* She was sousing pint-glasses in a tub, never looked up, but I got the signal-token all the same, Jemmy's no daw – *You make the moves, Jemmy, all them arrangements is entirely in your discretion, sir!* Then she looks up. Ever see what they call *the star foreknown* on the mortal human brow?'

Jemmy took a slug of tea, placed the cup – with gnarled care – on the floor, rose, removed a forlorn overcoat, black, ankle-length, held it up as you'd hold a picture for scrutiny. Closing his eyes, he spoke to the coat, to all who had ears to hear – 'Describe the wan. Well now, there's a job's going to drive me to the gable-wall. Still, I'll give it a go. Tidy, that's the first thing I'll say, tidy slip of a lassie, light on the toes, supple as the bee – are ye with me? Am I on the ball? *Correct!* Shape? She has all the shapes, was born to them, some be lucky, I could talk shapes till daylight but, come down to it in one swoop, it's the eyes in her head. Dazzlers, she's one dainty dazzler. And the hands, something about the hands, ever want to touch a hand? With one finger, even. Finger-tip. So's to be able to say – *I was there.* That was the present wit-ness's privilege and consternation? *Correct!*'

'The coat's wet,' the girl said. 'It's teeming still.' 'I believe', Jemmy bowed to the coat, 'we'll sample a step or two.' He took the coat out to dance, the wet black serge swayed responsively. Jemmy held it from him – the better to admire, drew it close – the better to caress. A waltz, his preference was for the waltz; foxtrot, tango, Lambeth Walk, would come in their season, for now pru-dent slow-waltz that circled the chair, cup on the floor, to uncer-tain hummed strands of 'Jeannie with the Light Brown Hair'. Every so often, Jemmy would stop dead, concentrate on the win-dow which gave on to the yard, hold breath, as suddenly relax, resume the waltz, sustained broken smile and your odd fantastic twirl of the feet as he coasted the bends.

Next episode, established. The boy took the girl out to dance, Jemmy and the coat, boy and girl, devising simple figures, sepa-rate and connected, conversing and happily silent, it could go on

13

forever but nothing was for long on Jemmy's clock. Except haste. Halted, he settled the overcoat carefully across the chair, petted it, thought – you'd venture – of a kiss, satisfied appetite with a long strig of the cigarette. The boy and girl, no longer dancing, watched the steam, drowsy tails of it, rising from the coat as the tended heat, blast from the range, worked on the weave. Jemmy addressed the bacon-hooks which pocked the high ceiling. 'Queen to behold,' he sang, 'On the pinnacle o' time.'

The calico Tom asked to be excused and was allowed into the night. Beyond the mearing the priest's dog howled. Jemmy put on the coat. Nudge for the cap, and – second nudge – return to previous inclination. Light one for the road. He shook his head at the range, advanced to the cat's spot, paused with his back to the heat, eyes on the mangle as if it had large questions to answer. The brute rollers, sodden with years, met his enquiry unblinking. 'Give me the horse,' the girl said. A skelp of rain hit the window. 'They don't, she don't, like to be kept waiting.' Jemmy made for the door, turned, hand on the latch, to reply to the girl, 'A white foal – I know where there's one friskin', white foal for yer bother – and you train-bearer, you on yer own, that content ye?' 'No but the horse,' the girl answered. 'Give me the horse, would you not?' 'White foal, *gearcaile*!' He spun on his heel, ghosted through the door, bicycle noises, the yard still.

Finally, rocks, water, she appears. Bowl of water now in her hands. She pours it over your head. It's 'truth-water'.

The team has been disgracefully beaten. There was one thing to be said for them, they were – plain for all to see – disappointed in themselves. To a touching extent, there in the rain, pleasantly dry rain which has bedewed many's the disaster in one or other of The Five Fifths of the Fissiparous Island. Few flavours so catching as despond. The supporters – on the brink of contumely – held back, stood there seeking to unravel conundrum. Never before has this gormless formation paused to mourn its own sway-backed incompetence. Was the dry rain, supporters probed, deluding them in especial? No, it was felt – ample spectrum – the mizzle stood as established decor, its curiously honest slant might not be impugned. Beneath it, humbled squad was in condign mourning.

And now a jump rare in the annals of competitive sport in this clogged hinterland – not unique, no, but assuredly rare – above all in the context of debacle, and we are, in this instance, crotch-deep in debacle. The followers – supporters – The Faithful – doughty battalion who had tholed much across decades – were moved to applaud. They saluted the arrant dismay of the defeated, a delicately formal spatter of applause rose, firmed, higher rose, found a neat platform of self-regard where it was free to consolidate, saraband taste to it, one commentator opined. The stately, it was explained, the dignity. Saraband furl came and went but the day wasn't by any means over, a finely liturgical and antiphonal *quelle surprise* was still blossoming, aspiring to – we soon had cause to speculate – the hardy upper air of the legendary.

It was the players' turn. And the players were finding – in no sluggard manner – what had eluded them during the game, invention, flair, esprit, such colours. Their response had an Attic simplicity. Stirred by the applause of the supporters, they applauded back. A salvo, takingly bold pivot to it. As that twist in the scenario manifested, even dullards on the terraces – as on the pitch – knew beyond question that here was the day of all their prayers. It had arrived, and, if it had, initially, registered as flummery, posturing, hysteria of the born victims, was now bold, brash, swaggering self-discovery. The next lunge was, depending on your angle of vision, a sinewy leap into the baroque or inevitable extension of an ordinary rhythm going about its ordinary day in a spirit of vagrancy, alfresco yearnings, extempore stitchings by Alice Benbow, she of the samplers, falsetto evening light and the shepherds' homeward trudge.

You have likely made the jump. The supporters began to weep. Openly, as people say. They shed guaranteed-genuine tears. (And, yes, keep in mind, delicate *ambages*, that dry rain still placing its restrained watermark on the drama.) The traffic could, at this point, go only one way. Reciprocity was Reciprocity Tyrannicus, with cornucopias akimbo. Meaning that the players now …? To be sure. The players – disgraced, redeemed (their dismay), the redemption sealed (the first applause), and twice sealed (their returning applause), and sealed again by the supporters' tears, now found Salvation's Harvest-Home in an answering outburst of tears. The famous old ground rang to the sound of weeping. And the slyly perdurable rain, whisper in the undertow.

We have arrived at the climax. Always, on these occasions, look out for our friend in the wheelchair and carrying (insurance) crutches, get to know him, he will frequently demand – and obtain – his fling in the annals. Inspiration of one of the Selectors – or, could be, his own maverick chutzpah, the invalid was paraded for a photo-'opportunity', that 'oopportunity' *en guimet* in deference to the referee's usage, dab of finesse surfacing in a report notable for its Byzantine illiteracy. The PM was present. Nothing happens without the presence of the PM, that's what Collectivity means. The expression on his face. Heraldic aphasic. *Per ardua ad* (where else?) *astra*.

A curtain instead of the usual doorway. That was a plus – from whatever donor. It had better be a plus. Door to the laden room

gone, curtain alluring. No doubt there was a catch. Wait. Qualifi-
er was visible, just about, find it – if you look carefully – there in
the louche hang of the curtain. And stillness that sheltered a braid-
ed caveat. Lump it. You must enter the room, you've waited long
enough, dread these moments passing and not returning. About to
enter the verifiable room of unverifiable portent, from under the
curtain, speaking in tongues, a famished gush of embers.

The Highest Counter

Once upon a time there was a barber called Taylor, and, consequently, a tailor called Barber, a blacksmith called White, and, accordingly, a mute called Argue, greengrocer called Pike, carpenter called Slater, undertaker Hope, tenor Crow, dentist Foot, beggar Cash, gelder called Love, butcher called Blessing, and thus, by decree, a watchmaker called Armstrong, Joe Armstrong, muscled and hirsute hoop of the strong arm, weal and woe of battle, clamour incessant, confronting the tiny wheels, filmy springs, and disappearing axles that were his *sotto voce* occupation and uncertain bread.

Enter – shop-window permanently shuttered – the dusk of Armstrong's premises. Admire, to your left, the tall counter, glass-topped, under the glass hundreds of watches, indistinctly labelled, condemned, asleep, forgotten – but brimming treasure-trove, witchery of dial, hands, silver, gold, blurred amalgams, you could devote all you possessed, or were possessed by, to their choiring stillness. Armstrong would have heard the door, would, when it suited, appear, lanky, bald, granny spectacles, merry grimace his unalterable greeting, and single sentence – *Spuds and rain and the Carrick train* – from which he had, since the day of its inception, gleaned small but sustaining portions of contentment.

Right inner corner of the cramped customer zone, a stoically frenetic grandfather clock. Its eye – you could tell, gloom or no – was on the high counter. As was yours. Measure that counter, mentally at least, every time you see it. Touch it every second time, let its mana nourish your initiate cells. It has claims to the fabulous, the mythic, nothing like it in these parts, it was from some previous patrician century or scarcely imaginable heroic age, boasted brass folderols and intricate panelling, invited and withheld, pacing shyly mature. Its central assertion of cachet was of a piece, had to do with its being stained by blood, blood which, in the event, had not been shed, and so had room to lave that counter in perpetuity, come and go, hypnotic and endearing.

An ordinary breakfast-time in the frowzy Armstrong kitchen. 'It's the salt makes the stirabout,' Joe had commented – ritual contribution – as he finished the first course. 'As stirabout the salt,' Sadie, the wife, advanced her melodic and biblical reply. The boiled egg followed – for Joe, Sadie did not eat eggs, and, a natural progression, was plagued by neighbours bringing gift eggs, hen-eggs, goose-eggs, duck, bantam, and once, Seán Sands, the stonemason, brought seagull-eggs from a summer watering-hole much in vogue. (Sadie disposed of surplus eggs by flinging them into the fields on her rare evening walks.) But breakfast. Joe, boiled egg consumed, is, for recreation, flaking the shell, a warm brown, deftly freckled, dropping the fragments onto the oilcloth – pallid cherry-blossom against off-white – which pro-tected the long-suffering deal. Sadie asked him to desist. He obliged, resumed the exercise. Sadie left the table.

Hours pass, not many. We know what Sadie was about in her bedroom or know in broad terms, she was remarked cleaning a window. Equipped only with rag and spittle – detail which gained general approval – she washed and polished the window over and over, bringing those willing panes to an unparalleled sparkling brilliance. Then, applying the same dedication, same rag and pliant spittle, she brought them back to their habitual dingy condition. Astute spectators – there were two, brother and sister, pensioners, next door – were entranced by the tale of Sadie's steady coming to visibility in that window, contrary re-duction to fog and mist, the bold connection between those paired movements and her life to come – this day, and across years in store.

Two o'clock, and Armstrong is behind the counter, turning the labelled watches in their sleep, petting his magnifying-glass. In the kitchen, dishes washed, Sadie puts on an apron, polka-dotted navy-blue, never before worn, selects her weapon, standard carving-knife, secretes it in her right wellington – she never wore shoes – and makes quietly for the shop. Sadie: soft-footed, reclusive, genetically morose, her people of the type 'inclined to cry when night comes'. She reaches the shop, short corridor from the kitchen plausive behind her. Joe, looking up, is struck by the calm in her demeanour. 'What were you at so?' he asked, not un-friendly. 'Cleaning a window.' 'Good woman yourself.' 'Then I dirtied it again.' 'Always the conservative.' 'Not always,' Sadie demurred. Joe didn't pursue it. Sadie stood there. 'Seán Sands might be glad of those goose-eggs the Lynch woman brought,' he threw out. 'Never,' Sadie said, 'they're for the fields.' No harsh note, everything nice and handy. 'Farmers won't thank you for upsetting the cows,' Joe conjured lightly, went on to prod, 'didn't they blame you for a shore taste in the milk from those seagull-eggs?' 'Cows don't eat them eggs,' Sadie spoke evenly. 'They just lick them, let them lie.' Joe enjoying this tasty pastoral cameo, Sadie reached into the wellington, still about her that inexpressible calm, limpid chasuble of her own inspired design.

'What went through your mind when you saw the knife?' Joe was asked by the many. 'What did you see – besides her level features – in that moment?' 'Flakes of that oul' eggshell,' he'd reply. 'Wet-day funeral, not much fuss or bother. Sadie by the grave – special permission, that face on her, exact same.' He confessed to some that he was overwhelmed – at the time, and ret-rospectively – by 'the justice of her cause'. Not immobilized. As Sadie moved to deal with him behind the counter – she must have seen him as trapped within – Joe stood up, weighed her. She was beside him. Blade descending, he vaulted – jumped –

flew – the counter, departed the shop, secured aid. Sadie made no resistance, smiled as she was taken away.

And in the twenty years of her stay in The Big House – where she died peacefully – was a model inmate. She had little to say but she said it often, and so it passed into legend. On the day of her arrival, and ceaselessly thereafter, she stated her one regret – she had never been to New Zealand. Some antipodal tremor in that *New Zealand*, and a primal conviction in the voice, ensured her a captive and enduring audience. As a young woman, she recited, the chance was hers, return ticket, all arrangements – courtesy of Aunty Eileen – comfortably in place for a three-month stay, but something had gone wrong, a death, an illness, some family dispute, and the plan crumbled. Now she'd never go. As she'd suspected – indeed known – at the time. 'It's the most beautiful country,' she'd conclude. 'In the known world.' Pause. 'And there to be seen.'

'All in,' the cry goes up, and the playing-fields of CWC – Carry on, Clongowes – empty, Pavilion melts, The Castle, The School, tower, parapets, flagpoles melt, leave not a thrawneen bar the silence beneficent, the summer, mallow quiet of evening, under your feet this earth that mourns its slain and buries its dead.

Take the deep breath, you're a big boy now. Could be. Those your legs? The Rector's? How beautiful, remote, billowy, burgeoning, the meadow. CWC, The Wood of the Meadow of the Calves. Of the White Cow, of the Grey White-Loined, stolen by their Cyclops from our Vulcan, Grey White-Loined would, if permitted, for as long as permitted, dispense milk for a whole province. Carry on, Clongowes! Feet up, Bective! A bear, big Mr Atlas lump of a bear steps out of the green ground. Hi, Hyacinth.

'He remembers everything, forgets nothing,' she told you once. Yes. 'Earth is the bear's ear,' she mentioned also, day you went with her to Armagh, Macha's height, O Neill Taoisigh-elect mounting the mare at Tullyhogue; in the Cathedral of Armagh a clatter of bambino-scale sculpted bears, Iron Age, earlier, releasing cello sounds. 'They used to have bears' graveyards,' she announced, 'but lately forgot to remember.' Bear now fornenst you, honest black block of a thing, *ora pro nobis* the beads of its eyes.

There was no threat. The bear had a football in the claws. 'Can you give me honey?' bear enquired. 'I've no honey here.' 'Somewhere else?' I hesitated – was seen to. 'Never mind,' said the bear, a night voice, far back in the cave. 'Still. Kill for a feed of it. Salty bone in the throat.' 'I'll go for honey.' 'Not now.' The bear danced, no Misha, no Sylvie, but an ungainly power, earth for trampoline, more lift than you'd have thought possible. The performing bear! And moved on to tricks with the ball, ball on the head, one shoulder, the other, between the legs, ball for chair, gravid ball as kittenish prey. The bear stilled. Fired the ball down the slope, went back into the homey ground.

Pursue the ball. The ball rolled a distance, the ball rejoiced in declivity, the winding path, the ball was your saucy mot, the ball was the heart of the rowl, the surround was altering, no more The Wood of the Meadow of the Calves, now there was scrub, thickets, the odd glade, the colours were apricot, peach, ivory, Thanksgiving brush, the ball came to a marsh, looked back at him, pleased it had led its pupil to trial destination.

The silence belonged to the other side. You are welcome, do not misbehave. Follow instructions. Leave behind your winkers, noseband, nosering, all your treasured harness, you may collect the lot on your way out, don't forget a *pourboire* for the porter. The marsh held no threat, a walk – if possible – of, say ten metres, would reach the ball. Step onto the marsh. Into the marsh. Sink. Sink to the waist but the walk wasn't a penance – permission, somewhere, had been given. Pick up the ball. Return to firm ground carrying the ball dispatched by the bear who'd kill for honey. Back on the solid – if such there be. The ball – business done – shed visibility. Look at yourself. From the *clábar* of the marsh, waist down, belly, privates, thighs, knees, calves, ankles below, clothing gone, entire lower-body a polished ochre cast. That shook you an' you're still rockin'. *Le vernissage*. For you. From them. For you.

The Order of the Bells

Bells. Bell. A bell haunts the boy. It glisters by his right hand, three cups on one stalk, a flourish of chimes, refulgent, compliant. The boy is, likewise, haunted by *The Order of the Bells*; three for the *Sanctus* – *Holy, holy, holy*; one before the Consecration, as the priest places fructifying hands above the chalice; brimming three for the Elevation, the raising of the host; and one on *Domini, non sum dignus*, as the priest summons the faithful to Holy Communion. There's a rich shadowy light busy about the bell, *Order of the Bells*. The boy has sounded the one, conducted the other, hundreds of times. That shadowy light has, far from diminishing, extended to cupola that resembles, is, the sky under which he, unsignificantly, moves.

Eleven o'clock mass on Sunday, event of the week, the church is packed. Six minutes past eleven on the creamily dogmatic wall-clock to the left of the altar. The boy's right hand assumes an independent fervour, gathers the bell, pauses, briefly, scatters three gallivanting chimes that leave in tatters the hallowed *Order of the Bells*. And yet. No harm. The priest quivers, lets it pass, faithful wonder, let it pass. The boy's parents, there in the Sanctuary, *parmi le beau monde*, shake themselves. The girl, she's there too, passes no remarks. The perpetrator, back to him, hasn't yet realized what he has set in motion. In short, from gaudy missal to far porch of the nave with its freakish and centripetal draughts, sabbath equilibrium holds.

Ponder this altar-boy's chosen hand. A carnival mischief,

seems, is pocketed in that hand. It hovers, miming innocence, flexes invisibly, waits. Seven minutes, approximately, of idle foreplay. And it acts again, gathers the bell, looses a rippling and mercurial chime that must – and does – cause concern. The priest flicks a glance, teeth in it. The faithful sit up. The parents intuit the worst, girl's taking her beads apart. The boy, the culprit – call him culprit – is still not certain what he's at. His security – everybody's – is that the mass will proceed, its ancient dignity will insist on that, mass is not interrupted unless by earthquake, tidal wave or vast civil commotion. But, in the mass's incapacity to stop lies the mass's Achilles' heel – some part of the boy knows that, no other reading possible, none examined.

Speculation is now active, cheerful besides. Who is this child? Oh, that child, that house, those grounds, trees, those parents, the girl. Odd crew, the best of days. Too bad about the afflicted one, only girl, horrid pity. Yes. The boy wasn't slow, anything but. Into himself, a bit, goes with the breed. Funny too what surround does to people, all that timber, couldn't be good for a body – and wasn't the front avenue said to harbour a ghost? Perhaps the ghost has possessed the child? A ghost loose on the altar. Anything's possible. Permissible. These days. The parents, feeling themselves under inspection, shrink, recover, shrink again, girl continues dismantling her beads. Hiatus. The ruffian world, keepin' an eye, mumblin' a prayer …

Sanctus, Sanctus … The *Sanctus* is nigh, propagating tension. The *Sanctus* will tell a great deal. The miching hand suspended, a bad sign, alert monitors estimate. The rest make nothing of it, everything will come right – God will see to it, His Holy & Blessed Mother, St Patrick. Someone. Anyone. St Jude. The hand moves, anticipating the Sanctus, frees a miscreant and unheard of four trills. Enough. All's now in the open, a relief, and a sickener. Priest flames, congregation hunch, parents in sync, girl continues the dismantling of the beads. The boy, truth be told, could faint, rejects the option. He begins to interest himself in the hand, *his* hand, wherever it is, somewhere in its own wild-cat heaven,

25

scheming more light-fingered and exemplary outrage.

Rev. B.C. Maguire, CC, celebrant, has a problem, several, but one immediately demanding: when to strike. The server, it's clear, is out of control – provocation (if there is any) irrelevant or it can be explored later. This question: strike now, in hope of shocking the child into orthodoxy, and live with the indignity, admission of indiscipline slobbering the steps of the altar – or brazen it out. That was a valid consideration, he, Rev. B.C., had known it called into play, and successfully. Ride the storm as if no storm there – and you may discover it thus curiously alleviated, in optimum contingency no longer storm, defused. Courageously, he goes for that, reaches for glory, but, almost at once, a wash of bile takes him – the affront, the intolerable affront of the antics *en train*. He rounds on the boy.

Tremendous turn here, an upstaging translucent hinge. The audience, it is now audience, gratefully on the hook, has perceived the curate's neck a conflagration, recognizes those flames must spread, sees the priest still, go rigid, and hold, humped, terrifying, for about ten alabaster seconds. *Action!* He wheels, 180 degree flawless swivel, rancid vestments in full sail, looks down on the boy, in that look distilled frustration, unbelief, nausea, fury and malediction, especially the last. A curse is being delivered. It has that appearance, certainly, there are those who wonder could the child, any child, survive this branding, for branding it is, you can in some reality, near or far, map fantastical or scabby morning pillow, smell the poor replicant skin, some imagine smoke, pray for the offender – who, mark this, and it was marked, is looking directly back at his judge and executioner with what the latter (his entitlement alone) will shortly describe as a 'quizzical expression', beyond interpretation, in the priest's view, except by experts in child lunacy, and that wasn't in his remit.

Mass doesn't stop and yet, *mirabile dictu*, it has. For all the foreground theatre, some take time to check on the distressed parents. The parents have taken the only road available, they've let down their honest heads, not physically, but in the rigorous illumined truth of the within. From this point, abject, they will sit it out. The girl is plucking hairs from the mink cape of the woman sitting directly in front of her (Sissy Sands), laughing under-breath the while. And the boy, the accused, outlaw usurper of the stage. The boy has this to say. Looking at the priest as the curse flew, brand seared, the boy is granted solace, wholly factual – yet fantastical: he's allowed to see, this is what penetrates and nourishes, he's permitted to see – flash-vision, through vestments, clothing, underclothing – a blistering mantle of grilled salmon-pink as it engulfs portly sacerdotal trunk and limbs. Flash – oven-sizzle, salmon-pink – *cut*. A painting. And forever.

Mass interrupted, mass proceeds. Much has altered. Hand and boy are one, the hand's omniscient, infallible, knows *ár lá* has come. And has leave. As is its custom, it lies low for a while, happy to pose, then goes wild, this is apotheosis, disregards the Consecration, firing two bold rounds when it's long past, denies deference to the Elevation, as to the raising of the chalice, as to the *Domini, non sum dignus*, and, in between times, is delighted to contribute double or treble chimes as whim directs, a *tour-de-force* incontinent that lives, strangely, off itself. The climax has come and gone, the priest has withdrawn from the contest, the congregation are beyond surprise or dazed or both. It will all end soon, says lemon sunlight from the eastern windows. And it does. A slow soon. *Ite, missa est*, dismal venom in the instruction.

Sacristy. The priest says nothing, refuses to acknowledge the boy's existence. The boy departs, arrives home – he must have flown, has no recollection of encounters en route. Grounds about him, he settles in a laurel – black bag containing singed surplice and soutane mute on his lap, there contemplates his precipitous curve of learning, emerges when he's ingested portion. He's livid, liberated, he's – to a rare pitch – himself. The father awaits him on the front avenue, there stands his father, the righteous, the harrowed, exposed. The girl – 'The bells were like Christmas,' she said over lunch – is playing under the holly; the mother, pruned cheekbones, cutting sprigs of lilac. 'What came over you?' the father asks. 'I don't know,' – boy's feet on the ground, hand larking in upper air, connected, disconnected, exuberant, of age. 'You don't know?' 'No, I don't know.'

Grandmother in the Tree

Sent to gather *brosna* under the mother-beech, he relished the job
– more than anyone in the house; the father wouldn't stoop to it
(could be the back was at him), the mother would but, watching
her, you'd say, 'She's cajoled a way of gathering *brosna* without
soiling her fingers,' it seemed to lift into her hand as the hand
neared; the girl would engage but gave him the sense that, in
some former existence, she'd tasted enough of the stuff for several lifetimes, loved its crumbly runes, didn't have to bother herself with them this time round. He pooched in the beech-mast,
the leaves, let wafts of compost imbue him, cellar bounty,
ripeness of ripeness. *Brosna*.

Shouting. That was the grandmother in the tree above him.
'Lie on his head or he'll break a shaft,' she was screeching –
singing more, fragments – *brosna* – constantly spilling out of her
memory-box, to be explained sometime or never, always taking
root. She'd been around a long time, educated early. 'I cooked
myself, only Universitee.' Never graduated, she'd add, wasn't so
foolish, would from the clay, accept, *merci, merci,* parchments descending. He climbed the tree, found her well up the trunk,
windburned, cosy in her skin. She looked through him but with
him. 'How're you?' Habit of hers to ask questions answers to
which she already possessed, she was didact, shawled, woollen
socks dangling from the filly feet. 'Middling – not to boast of it.'

She'd taught him to consider replies, her notion being that all
haste was of the Adversary, noise of time inaudible in the ham-

mer of tongues for long spaces now.

'And you've the *brosna*?' He handed her the bundle. She examined the decaying twigs, connoisseur tingle, selected one, peeled it with the extraordinarily long nail – sulphate-green, runny blues – she'd allowed develop on her right index finger. 'What's *it* for?' 'To peel spuds the next famine.' She licked the peeled strip, put it in her mouth, chewed it – she had all the teeth, and swallowed the pulp, mottled light coming and going across her younger face, always younger, she could be twenty, was likely a hundred. 'Not bad.' She gave him a piece. He chewed and ate. 'Well?' 'Tastes like wood.' 'What'd you expect?' He let that go. 'What've you to do, what'd I tell you?' 'Eat the tree.'

Eat the tree. Of all the riddles – and she a pure brew of riddles – this was the trickiest. Eat bread, spuds, fish, flesh or good red herring, but eat the tree? And suppose you did eat the tree. 'Then you'd know the next move.' 'No other way to know it?' 'You'd like it for free, wouldn't you?' she'd rapped. 'His Highness a superior suckling-palate, dainties of another sort'd suit, that it?' 'How'll the tree – eaten – tell me the next move?' 'It knows. Eat it, you know.' He still had bother with the notion, not least because of the wicked sour and rasp in the wood juices, you could be dining in Tokyo or Kyoto or by night on the Limpopo. 'Look,' she snatched the *brosna* from his lips, 'don't bother your powdered arse. Stay stunted if that's what you want.' 'It's not.' He made an act of faith, she clocked its pulse, gave him back the contentious morsel.

They went for a walk in the tree, she crooned, her hand in his assurance of fair footing, views, rinsed air belting the lungs. He knew, pair of them strolling a massive southward-stretching limb, they were bound for the idol, that was her word for it, a lump growing from the limb, size of a head, human head in the making. Bright creation if it ever came to be, you'd swear to that, knowledge somewhere inside you, coming off the tree, a promise. They'd been attending to it this while, visiting it, handling it, watching it firm to shape, borrow features, expression, even, expression of relief, he'd call it, but *layered* expression, to be honest, and layers playing musical chairs, or ladders, so that, soon as you'd decided 'relief', that layer gave way to another – 'gratitude', say – and that, in turn, to another – 'certainty', that to 'warmth', that to 'excitement', tomorrow another day and not a bite out of it yet. The idol. *Tomorrow*, his name for it.

'Good-day, sir.' There was the idol, the leaves petting it, forming head strong today, coming sweetly into itself, hesitations of a smile. Man's head, you'd guess, young man's. 'Will it take him long?' 'To come out? As long as it takes. Then, could happen, he'd dart back in, never show.' 'Why'd that be?' 'Hasky weather drives them back in – just like people. In ways.' 'If he shows, will he talk?' The boy drifted a finger along dim track of lips in the emerging face. 'He'll talk all right. Understand what he's saying is another dollop.' 'English, will he have?' 'No telling. Mostly his crowd talk without words. Don't need language. Except when it suits.'

She squatted to pee – he'd no idea what she drank to provoke pee in such quantities, she must have a bladder like a Zeppelin or come from Greenland whales on the mother's side, times he'd wager she was built to spout pee from any orifice she pleased, spout, gush, swamp the vicinity. And it was warbling pee, reels, slides, spoons, bones, trombones on the tear as she pissed for minutes on end, laughed with the flow, closed her eyes and moaned, bereaved organ, listen, *a mhic*, slap of the piss down through the branches, pigeons scuttling for cover, one, insulted, fled the tree, and, shunt in the shindig yielding a window, he glimpsed the ash, ash with secret store, butter wouldn't melt. His eye flew to that cleft, the one in particular that needed watching, carried a riff of apprehension. It was all right. The cleft was idle, harmless.

'Got off light, did ye?' She rose from her squat, dropped the skirts. 'Give that eye another tack, child.' He let on not to have heard or, if he had, not to have understood. She'd have none of

it. 'Give – I know your duck-an'-weave – that scarified eye another tack, learn sweet damn all watching with the small of yer
back.' He looked again at the cleft in particular, saw – after a
truce second – the shell appear like an old friend and vehicle of
danger, appear and perform, the mouth opening and shutting, to
invite, to grip, then open – not wide, little more than a slit, but
sufficient to envelop him once more with its there-and-gone
vorous pink-flesh, juiced and mobile. 'I love the madness in
trees,' she fired in the dig. 'Pitch off those duds.'

Colour returning – that shell, its contents, could tap him at
will – he threw off his clothing. She dressed him in leafy branches, head to toe. 'Come back when you're fit.' He took off, roamed
the tree, other trees, the grounds, dressed in the branches. Several states at once adhered. A kind of invisibility, for example; seeing but unseen, you blended, swam in the green. Also, you were
lighter on the spot, stones lighter. And you didn't walk, didn't
have to, *leap* was the game, leaping how you breathed, twigs – on
the feast day – would spill from your ankles, leaf or two for a
tilly. There was fear in it too, this wasn't customary travel.

Eat that fear, she'd counsel, and you'll shit health. His fear in
the foliage dress had to do with invitation, scope of invitation.
There was the grandmother note, note – under the timber sours –
of eating the tree, note of travel in this learning guise. Scope.
Scoops of scope. Too many doors open. Space too much, depth
and width. Centre and circumference yo-yo in the rain, centre
everywhere, circumference nowhere, sit down, Euclid, and wipe
your snot. Yes. But a side of him, fat flitches of him, would rather
be at home minding himself. Or the girl. Calico Tom. Tongs from
the fire. Watching the mother purse her face, father rattle change
in his pocket. Comfort of come-day, go-day, God send Sunday.
The hammock. The snore.

Still an' all. Liberty the lap of the grandmother, dowser's rod
the long fingernail. 'Can I have another look at that nail?' He was
taking off branches, putting his duds back on, high in the tree.
'Bite it, maybe. That what you want?' She let him examine it,

never the same twice, myrtle-green this time, and blue-black, one horny talon, touching it was like touching a live wire, doses of crackle, watch it, Mister. *To peel spuds the next famine.* 'I'll grow one like that,' it pleased him to rise her. And she rose like barm. 'You'll grow one the like of it! Gelangourathat, ye sparrow-fart *is glan do thóin bheag Ghaelach*, ye were reared on the hind-tit and yer stuck with it always, it'll follow you like a crab-weasel tucked under your lug, hiss whenever you'd pretend it wasn't, bloat to a swaybacked buck and ate you for greeshkeens some day you're prancing your airs. It's the hind-tit croups the brain-pan!' Her snarls followed as he went down the tree-stairs, exhilarated him, that bile of hers an old baptism of longing.

'Don't forget the bearskin rug I left over the end of the bed' – her shout from a distance. Parthian.

Knockbride, Bridget's Hill, Magna Mater in the spring, there's a bog, the original red-bog, not many of them left, the colours – amethyst, tanbark, cerulean blue, seduction's stronghold there to the left of the road, and the dwarf appears with purple flower in hand – botanical mystery, unlisted, beyond categories the purple sings. I should accompany the dwarf, explore the bog, but no – for some reason, not now, perhaps hereafter, the dwarf's eyes understand, no comment, old dog for the hard road. 'I'm for Monaghan,' I explain, 'The Thicket.' His gaze has knowing, could say but doesn't – 'Were it Monaghanoose itself, The Hiding-Place of the Deer' – still it isn't, it isn't, and what is underdone cannot be helped.

A gooseberry-bush. Adult lore, child lore. Adult crepitus: play gooseberry, would you? Chaperone – ah, chaperone – an older especially or married woman to escort a younger, keep an eye, praetorian, lest should befall what might … (Last night's circling shadow of a cat was chaperone transubstantiated, dubious addition the subtraction. Her circling shadow! Let bad news wait, it might improve.) Back to the gooseberry-bush, childhood icon invoking Robert Louis S's *Child's Garden of Verses* (RLS known to the Samoans as '*Tusitala*' – 'teller of tales' – *Weir of Hermiston*, last novel, blew him out of it), recall that bush, near the swagger of pampas-grass – sired, surely, by Rudyard K cantering from some deep defile, silk of pampas secure in memory, current gooseberry-bush a sight for sore eyes, stripped bare of her bachelors (even), drab runt of a thing now, eloquently, let's say, in denial, those thorns lack bite, ne'er a leaf, gird your lathered loins, there's more, more, under the mobled bush your white bird lies, dove-size, flattened and still, how'd that happen? Insecticides? Predators unknown? Natural causes may be ruled out, the bird is (was) in her prime. Should you report this death? To whom? That poor stillness without stirring a feather makes a dent, still, a tough ould station, your attention is, politely, drawn to the assembled flies, o, man, there interposed a fly, dozens, you could have well done without this visit to the garden, and no, you may not leave, this silence has tentacles, the white bird, yours, dove-size, is at once itself and effigy, those flies – they could turn metal, any second, shrapnel, stand by for contusion, traveller, the cruciate ligament in these travails is *calme, du calme*, there is the danger of the congealed, granted, not to speak of petrifaction in dim zones beyond, and yet *du calme*, mark, lying by the bird, sort of hidden in the grass, several gooseberries (could the bird, your white bird, have o-dee'd?), the berries look tasty in that liquid way they have, brimful, seed and juice, fuzz of the delicate container, one of those berries especially, berry in full sail, holds you, get your mitts on that, stoop, fingers agile, pick it up, pocket, and get out of here, gormandise at leisure, fruits of the earth, Adam delves, Eve spins – like a teetotum, RLS just heeled over, the white bird compels – as your first corpse, remember, bird here is kin, must be, to the bird, white also, who hammered your bay window, inviting, looking onto the lake, the glass, proud insulator, would not give way, regular wall of window, imperturbable grown, bird, accordingly, seagull size, bounced off the glass, undeterred came all night long, brass-and-cymbals, retired at dawn, returned – your aviary of predilection teems happy returns, returned before long as the hawk high up there, now descending, hen-harrier, looks like, pheasant colours, that range, owl-face, across several days – how slow a sentry you can be when you put your mind to it – over days its sniper eye measures the snake, toy, drowsy on the table by the window (you must learn the snake, take that bite), a window again, your life's a tale of windows, reinforced glass, that wire-mesh is highly spoken of, yes, the hen-harrier dived by dusk to greet the snake, they too must meet, it's written, but let the clash be for real, hen-harrier breaks her neck on the defiant glass – WHUMP – you rush out with a bowl of water – to concoct a blessing – wash the remains – your maculate hands – next morning hen-harrier's mate, long tail a tremble, meets you outside the door, is waiting for you on that convenient telephone-wire, gives, economical by nature, you one look, paunches you, leaves, these are not cheerful tidings, there are some up ahead, don't blink – nor cheerful the climax (if climax it be), the hawk substantial follows, eagle size, perhaps eagle, yes, go for that – imagine dove, seagull, hen-harrier, rolled into this exalted messenger, positioned directly overhead, supple your hard neck, Captain, fifty feet up, bulk and presence to stop a platoon, where the boreen meets the main drag, they pick their venue, there floats His Highness, flying on one wing, hovering – but could fly to Samarkand, if so minded, today a visitor for your agape devotion, hangs there, banner, so marvellously balanced, that single outstretched wing transparent, nothing to hide, look, through it the blue above, moving clouds.

Things You Might Notice About Her

Gaol. She was never shut up. At that time, in that place, in most places, it was the custom to tether in a corner those lacking the full eye, encourage them to keep indoors, cultivate absence one way or another. McGinnity the shoemaker's daughter, an instance, was only ever seen through a window. There was a daughter in the Fletcher Tinley's whose skin was scaled, she was allowed out in the dusk, always heavily clothed, veiled and gloved in heights of summer – a name existed for what she had which no living soul could remember. And there were other examples, numerous and well-hidden. That was never the case with her (except once, we'll come to it), she was given free rein, the grounds were hers, roads in the immediate vicinity, the streets, and some houses, shops, of the town. There might be a stain, there was, the one girl, such a pity, but she would not be gaoled.

Gait. She had a way of walking that was entirely her own. Other children, girls and boys – look at them rude in their bodies – they just walked from here to there, and back. It was not in her to walk, and, certainly, it was not in her to run – there was no hurry – why should she hurry? (She had never been seen to run, what a sight that might have been, see her going flat out, breasting the tape, first in the race, and the hair flying ...) Fact was, she swayed, so she did, from place to place, an arm coasted independently, she looked only vaguely towards where she was going, her steps had a disorder that almost created an alternative order, at times did, and then you might be willing to concede that she was fetching the beat from far within, had found a dance, found a tune, hers, nobody else's, that showed, eluded, returned to dwell in the sanctuary ear.

Margin. She had picked up at an early stage – the line of fire taught her more nor her prayers – that she was of the margin, there must abide. Watch it ten thousand times, it was always shock to meet that idiom in performance. Take, for example, children at play, on the favoured lawn or in the trim garden west of the house, visitor children, she has undercover companions, there they are alive and waiting. You'd see her appear – out of a bush, the laurel, the lilac – appear and hover and enter the scramble of play and play-act as participant but never for long, some force would pull her back to the margin, and a customary see-saw would shape, the other children, girl-children, be sure, showing great time for her, minding her in their simple trust, wishing her persistently into the action, that shy drag towards the margin working contrarily, until – where is she? She's elsewhere. The game goes on.

Speech. When she spoke, which wasn't often, she had a *grá* for long silences, but when she spoke, the moment she ventured past simple statement – *I will, I won't, the dog's at the door* – and into, say, leaps of the metaphorical – *Put wheels on crabs, to listen to him* – a rank colour of the imitative was visible, audible, you knew, registered at once, that it wasn't in her to digest words, rejoice with them, but, she had, still and all, caught some charge that sustained, the hint of some code, system of barter, incantatory wiles, and she'd lay claim as well as the next – *That new iron spits like a gander … A flood at the door that'd turn a mill … No absolution for whipsters …* It wasn't parroting, quite, some bravura tint took it beyond parroting but, if you didn't know and cherish her, you'd probably call it parroting, no doubt many did, upfront finaygle her bashful admission ticket to the party. Imitation of another hue: the odd foreign phrase could set her drunk. *Merci beaucoup* she took a fancy to one autumn, held on to it vertiginously. *Merci beaucoup!* And *Dominus vobiscum* had its protracted reign.

Sweets. Her offering of sweets. It must be that the itch of selfishness had been given no room in her, everything belonged to everybody. Bag of sweets outstretched, present from somebody. 'Take your pick, there's lots.' And she meant it, it ran with her breath. There was some fabulous generosity in the gesture, lightness in the hand, nothing would cling to it, she was the creature of no property, her store was yours.

There were weathers they shared, he and she. Call the first of these the weather of the gale. An October gale from the southwest howled and thumped and ballyragged the house and outbuildings, and on his way to school the boy had to climb over thirty trees, fir, Douglas, and spruce, Sitka, mostly, which had been uprooted in the darkness and were now blocking the back avenue, fairy-tale skittles. In awe of the gale he stood quiet a long time, counting and recounting the fatalities, and then a murmur told him she was there ahead of him. He caught her voice, she was talking to herself, to the strewn timber, exact words inaudible, but he followed the sound and found her close to the gate, studying the crudely exposed roots of a victim fir. 'Strings and guts,' she pointed, spell on her. And made him accompany her on a tour of the succession of hiant roots, still whimpering guts. She'd gather and pocket crumbs of clay at each site.

And honour, besides, forge of the frost. Because the town was the highest or nearly above sea-level anywhere on the island, and, additionally, of the brusque hinterland, January could be relied on to sculpt and solder, work wicked scrolls of white and blue and surly greys. One morning of her birthday (18 January, as stated), she was posted missing and he went to look. The frost was black inside the white, the pure black-white juice, annealed. The grounds, the perpendicular world, had turned to metal, iron, luxuriantly wrought, pride in the arabesques, tender arrogance in the barb. You could hear the trees ache to keep themselves whole, cough and groan and sometimes snap. He knew where he'd find her, in that brush by the stream which in summer imaginings sheltered a yellowhammer, pocket as far as possible from the house, mearing the road. He wandered to it, queer din of the frost under his boots, all birds dead or banished, and found her – child of winter, angel of the blast – forager and sturdy under a young sycamore, fingering an icicle that hung from its lowest bough. She heard him coming, looked, broke off a piece, extended it to him from a mittened hand, small red fingers votive in the task. 'The water's choked,' she announced. They looked at the frozen stream, fragilely anchored, by whorls in the glass, detained shadows, eerily flotsam whites, the story limbo'd now, but remotely listening for the liberation hour. They held each other then, as before a lamp, grew cold about the lugs, went back up the slope, across the imprisoned lawn, and into the still house together.

Note, too, downpour, summer downpour, she drew him, convertite, to these picnic washings. There was an old schoolmaster over the road – no doubt she'd met him – who came abroad only to the beat of the downpour. Her like addiction no castigation could lessen. With the swallows and the sow, she could tell weather from the colour of the wind. He watched her fling on a torn raincoat this summer day, went with her down the avenue. The coat was simply an antic flag of convenience, easily shed, now shed as the heavens parted and the deluge arrived. She led him to the centre of the lawn. They stood there, faces upturned, mouth-bodies drinking the teem, a drink and a washing like none other ever known, rain sang in the thrapple, made liquid the joints, did away with skin. They were rain with the rain. After, she shook herself like a collie, pawed the drenched dress, looking for herself. 'What's inside the water?' she enquires. 'The well,' he tried. She looked past him, frankly. 'What's inside the well?' God knows. The stone? One well he knew and had often studied – it was on the Ballinamoney Road – a stone looked up at you from clear water, cracked stone, odd symmetry to the slew of zany cracks running, you'd believe, from the flag's precise centre. 'What's inside the well?' He gave her, undine, a rainy kiss.

Omission: white bird, goner, hanging from branch of a tree near the barn.

Overheard – The Warrior's Tale. He trained with The Old One in folds of the wood, she passed on her tricks. An apt pupil. She wasn't one for soother-talk but he knew she was content with progress, chirpaun to fineladyouare. Time for the next jump. 'How fast can you run?' 'Faster than anyone.' She landed on his back – this had happened before – but he'd always been able to unseat her, now she was stitched to his shoulder-blades, the tough legs a belly-band. 'Have to be dug out of you,' she crowed. Well, we'd see, so we would. He took off, ran so fast by the time he stopped nothing left of her bar the two shinbones. Erect in his fists. 'I should be painted this minute,' he said to the day. Snigger from a bush. He'd a half-notion he'd found himself a slithery brae, didn't all the same give a damn, pitched the shinbones into an available lake – she thrived on lakes, and he knew it. He relished the parting, almost a wooing, curve, serendipitous, of the first (right) shinbone, high-flier, seabird, dipping, and – velvety splash – sipping the water, mulberry, bog-lake, and gone. Then, hand now jolly, venturesome, repeat, more finely tuned, with the left, it sang cheeky farewells, javelin, *a capella'd* its backward look, but, young buck well-hung, menace didn't cross his mind. (In the nature of things, expect, wager, he'd one day parade authority on shinbones – 'Can't be too cagey with shinbones,' the podium, the mike, the melancholic young. 'They're not thigh-bones, not collar-bones, they're shin-bones, know the speckler fire, the ground, water. A question of the proximate.' The lame savant.) Worm in the left shinbone did the damage, or as well put it that way as any other way, right? Going about his father's business, he began to catch signals, blips on the screen, tinnitus of the capacious small hours. From a conspirator soon, he knew what was cooking, and the shack not far from the lake where he'd find her. Didn't knock. He'd spare them both that charade. Pushed open the lice-bitten door, looked in. Not a stim of light. Whinge of a match in the room beyond, jig of her lighted candle. And she called – 'Well?' He said nothing, tongue a knot. 'Well?' Noise behind him. A boy put his head in the door, six or seven, put him: a sprig, with cherry, glowing, pops out of his mouth. 'How fast can you run?' She was calling from within. Her Indoors. 'Hey, Big Fella, how fast can you run?'

Addendum – Warrior knew he was going to die when he dreamt two pup seals, fresh from the wave, coming to suck at his breasts, milk-laden. They were his offspring, however that might be. Was. And he knew a participation hitherto out of his reach, progenitive, petted the seals, shine of them, satiny bundles, muzzle-tug slap at his nipples, it came to him that he'd arrived, he was on the move, it was time to swim. He slept. The seals sucked until they too slept. All slept. Thus his departure, to muted clamour of the shelving shore.

That cherry. 'Crush the red flesh to reach the hard stone.' 'Again, please.' 'Crush the red flesh to reach the hard stone.' Child's eyes peeled him. 'Why so sad? What's the problem?' 'I am.'

Dig Right, Dig Left

The town was split. We were one crowd, they the other. They had different names, faces, ways of walking and ways of talking, different halls, churches, banners, wars, memorials, days of commemoration, different hats and ties and shining shoes in which to admire themselves grimly. We were ourselves, they were different – Bells and Cranstons and Porters and Parrs and Rowantrees and Jamesons and Hagues, where had they come from – and urged by whom? Scotland was mentioned, and England – but England would have been mentioned anyway, and, in the matter of crowned prophet, twisted elect, there was no competition, Luther won pulling up, his only rival one Knox, sometimes visible as adjutant to the German Satan. Herr Luther. Nailing damnations to a cathedral door, couldn't shit, in the end – bad luck to him – choked on his own vomit.

Maybe it was a good that they were different – the possibility was sometimes floated from the pulpit, provocatively tickled, maybe that kept everyone awake, the opposition, the bad – if you like – example, the night, noon, and morning *presence* of the others, looking stubbornly the other way, doing the other thing – what better goad? Only, in the end, something to talk about. It wasn't a benefit. We all knew it wasn't because, plain on the platter, it would have been a much better world, more on the road to settings of perfection, if they also had possession of the truth, if they also had been given that gift, grace, path to The One. They hadn't. And so be it.

And, by Christ, it was in their mugs, you didn't have far to look. They, as established, had a face, we had a face, at once a natural state of affairs, of appearances, but also eternally strange – perhaps because, the boy pondered, faces are eternally strange anyway, demand, and defy, reading. The face they had was sallow to fair, firm in the jaw, broad in the brow, well-fed, convinced, on the alert, and that from some steps up the ladder. It wasn't a face that sang or wept – unless in private but that was unlikely, singing was never heard from their abodes, weeping neither, no bright banshees for those who lack the *O* or *Mac*. Our face. That wasn't so easy, describe your own mug, like being asked to find word for the nape of your neck you can never see. Our face was, we'll say, dark – by contrast, certainly. Fond of shadow. Fond of the rain. Bladder very near the eye. Sang intemperately. Full of shouts. Mutters.

But leaving aside names and faces – if, for one moment, you could – *Above* or *Below* was the burning debate, who'd go where? Consider: there was no bother accepting that Gamble and Hester Hague, girded and girdled blackest of the black, would paddle the sinks of hell but what of Heather, what of Denise, the beautiful Hague daughters? Untouchables, they glowed, their sallow complexions demanded constant attention, their fluent progress from house to school (their school) and back excited supine glands, Heather and Denise – were they destined for Below? We never spoke to them, they nurtured a frilled silence. Stand-off – porous. All right, we had our own incomparable beauties, a sufficiency, more on the way. We didn't complain. All the same. Heather and Denise, their multiplying endowments, touchable untouchables, no litany they did not – and sinuously – colonize. We prayed for their redemption knowing they carried our salvation.

Meanwhile, all's in equilibrium, split but in equilibrium, no need of sleepless nights, could go on forever, must, it's the world, stretches into future pluperfect, reliable as The Bank of England, Old Lady of Threadneedle Street embroidering the approved, Carrickmacross Lace another version of same, Ark-low Pottery or Wedgwood or Beleek, known shapes smooth from the wheel, and decorated to please, generation unto generation. Willow Pattern, it was there too, in the scales, the balanced scales, and finely. They could not be disturbed. They must. They were. One day, week, month, season, it all came upset, there was no equilibrium, not the colour, never would be again, bowl broken. A young one of ours, young woman, the word ran, had, just like that – like tasting a cup of tea – married one of theirs. That and worse. She had converted in the process, gone over, was now one of them. She'd turned.

There's a boil, suppose, on your hand: the question always – 'Is it *bealing*?' The town was *bealing*. Rather, our side was. The like had never been known or, if it had, so long since that it didn't matter. The apostate – that was the word – was a Duffy, Liz Duffy, servant-girl in Cranston's, now mistress, Duffy pack always knew the oiled grin, old bedroom route, first brat on the way, droves to come, sabbath screechers and the seed of more, it would come back to her on the wind. People crossed the street to avoid her, turned corners, counted pebbles, spoke into their collars or buttoned their lips. She was called slut, whore's melt, and rip. Eggs were set to rot for her in clay.

That wasn't all. The boy knew her to see, this young woman, Liz Duffy, and it was his fate – for confused good or ill – to meet her one day, week after she'd proclaimed herself. It was on the street, beside the thriving premises – hardware – she'd married into. Enter Liz from behind a van – she'd been in conference with the van-man, copper piping, coil on coil, flamed on the footpath – up she pops as the boy's passing and they've met, both agree to it, she takes him on, he sways in the sudden of it, the suction, amaze. Liz: outcast, she stared down into him, stirred so that her breasts moved to a sonsy tilt, grinned, showed him the plump of her tongue, waltzed on. She didn't give a damn. All she gave was – a twelve-gun salute – to herself. For his benefit. *A chroí!* Like a lick? Better nor ice-cream.

Plump – inundation. The staggers. He refused lamb's tongue for dinner that evening, picked at the nerve, ungovernable power, in those chatty legs. And picked more. And was relieved to find that, in no time, Liz was becoming history. The town had been split – but in equilibrium. Equilibrium was now the echo, far away, of another dispensation. In the new mandamus, every-thing was moving at carnal impetus, how did you keep up? Stand by for a hanging; in crooked hindsight, it seemed there'd always been someone about to be hanged, another young fellow in Belfast Friday. The town tightened, had been on a wind-up for days. Our side. Theirs. You could catch killing in the air, bitter creak, unforgiving. Fine, let them hang him, young Tom Wil-liams, they had the rope, the gallows, the dirty skills (always ex-pert there, remember Red Hugh, the poisoned slipper, Salaman-ca), but that didn't mean his passing would go unwept, unho-noured. All shops would close as a mark of respect. Traders were so informed – 'mark of respect for a brave soldier sentenced to die for heroic action in defence of noblest principles.'

Count-down. Tight and tighter, narrowed mouths, eyes, ar-teries not far behind. A certain few on their side, easily named, would spit on the request – instruction. The old firm. Very good. Sanctions would be applied, details on demand, free of charge – but such elaboration scarcely necessary, sanctions meant – do your sums. Nine o'clock on the eve, the town was a knot, blood finding it hard to run, carbolic puce binding cheek and jaw. It would go to the wire, that was the dance, long in the learning.

The clock ticked. It was down to three now, steeped true-blues and God Save Our Stuttering King. These heroes would not put up shutters, deepest regrets, but they'd more to do, goods to sell, public awaiting, trust to be honoured (since hon-our and honouring were so much to the fore). Thank-you. Cer-tain needful matters were, once more, patiently explained, set on the table, no murk. Bell and Jameson yielded. Rowantree, the butcher, stood firm until past midnight. A taste of his own spa-cious refrigerator, fine slabs of beef and mutton (one mournful ox-tail, it was reported) for company, cleared his mind of cant. Can and can't. The lad was hanged. The shops closed. Town sat there, all wired up, terror to breathe.

And no brake. From a wedding, summer celebration in Mountnugent, twenty miles west, snap of gunfire upsets the day. Detectives, knowing the gathering would draw certain parties on a certain wanted list, had invited themselves and their weapons to the feast, wedding did not, contrary to popular belief, bestow exception, a war now in progress, old war on a modern footing, guns latest automatic, the red handshake plentiful, it was now and venomous and back tomorrow for more. Birds, dogs, horses and milch cows shifted – and were seen so doing – to give the combatants room. Bridal veil on the heavy dog-days' air, confetti, blessings galore, poteen from Mullaghmeen, speeches with apt references to the executed, the murdered, the lacerated in mean depots fashioned for such barbarity. Bee at the window. The invited uninvited arrive with their uncomplicated demands, pistols start to sing against the come-all-yiz, bride white to her shift, two dead, one detective, one the wedding-party, prisoners, an escapee across the field, ditches, drains, boat on Sheelin. Funeral arrangements later.

He will take shifting. 'Must have my thought where the music is,' I speculate. Blank. My Hyacinthus is impermeable. 'Buddha is conversation,' I try. He's thinking – 'What's the half-time score?' Keep at it, so I float – 'Stork finds the thermal / Swift sleeps on the wing.' But he's not a twitcher – or, ornithologically, stork and swift lack cachet, that be it? He needs – in the lees of Mammy's soup – the exotic, the halcyon, halcyon hatching halcyon days. I put a pencil to his lips, let it play there. He tracks the pencil – might be a wand now. Those lips, tacit lips of the braggart Celt. Jesus, he'll take shifting.

Go for it. Lottery. Present myself in green, Italian blue, Oriental red, sack over my head, hair over my eyes ('Hair over your eyes, I've difficulty – it's curious – hearing what you say.') In lightly falling snow. Nyet. I try black – with brilliant colours. Or how about right foot lamed? I stalk naked – pubic fuzz a wilful ruby, show a haunch – flecked with blood (that stopped him, he recovered quickly), I bring him an apple (accepted), whitethorn in blossom – tinged with purple ('Unlucky – were you never told? – to let whitethorn under the roof.'), I try pouting breasts, my hair pageboy to bestow on him bear's pelvic basin, scrubbed bony throne (he tucks it in a wardrobe, 'Mind that wardrobe,' I warn), I arrive face upside down, parade with shit on my bare ass – 'Tristan used to lick it clean.' (Astringent smile, in five minutes he'll be doling his Tristan/Iseult rhapsodies, has all the versions, knows the rhymes, Gottfried von Strasbourg an old butty, quotations spin – 'A man, a woman. A woman, a man.' Wipe yourself, would you, like a good lassie?) I get myself pregnant – by him – he's delighted. But don't, Iseult, get carried away, don't fall overboard, sharky waters, Sister. I propose he give himself a long sleep while hanging upside down. Looks at me, bless him, rancorously.

Interim verdict (no surprise): this boyo equates passion with laces.

In a weak moment – O, leafy yellowness, you create for me – he will allow me to cut his hair. It isn't that I'm vengeful, want to trim his sails, want to, I don't know, I'd been waiting for this. That's all. I seat him centraleee. Already, I remark, without comment, he's gone uncharacteristically morose. We fear the worst! Old olive at the gill, hints of that. 'Why so pale and wan / Will, if looking well can't move her / Looking ill prevail?' The implements are, prestidigitously, to hand. Was I carrying them all this time? Nothing complicated. A scissors – sharp. A comb – metal, it turns out. And I like that. Sheen. The bit of class. The house has gone impatiently still.

Aon, dó, trí. STOP. He's changed his mind? Signor Mobile. Yes. No. Shouldn't a shampoo come first? Digression granted. Hair washed. Ready to go. Again, I seat him centraleee ... 'Much off?' I enquire, humble handmaiden, anxious to please, ever. 'I place myself in your hands,' he – I was waiting for this – yields to his weakness for the expansive gesture. And – as I scalp him – he's gloomily passive, an effect – plus affect – of the grandstanding, I've studied it in him, *avancez*, he will now – he must – he does – chew the doped grapes of fantasy – nothing is happening, or the reverse is happening, o, the mind has mountains, insure your sherpas if you'd look twice at The Matterhorn, he's given a close, the closest, front, back, and sides, with, subject comatose, tonsure flung in, Hibernian Monastic Nouveau, ear-to-ear band, livid skull-divider, adze-head. Then – no pause for breath – I clip the tufts of blond hair rearing from his incisors. He jolts awake. 'Didn't know you had those?' Jawdrop. These blithe intuitives! The sensate world no piddling concern of theirs – let her roll – this way The Ziggerat, that way The Skaggerat! 'Have a look.' I supply a mirror. He has a look. 'You have arrived, Benan.' 'Benan?' 'St Patrick's Chief Gauleiter in the alleged peaceful conversion of The Island.' I took pictures. That dismay had to be ambered, archival purposes. He didn't say much for a week. Then he said nothing. Opened the mouth. Left it at that. Bar a note, simply, asking me to leave. 'Better for all concerned.'

He must see everything through glass – this be the verse you grave for him. So how about a round window, portholey, in a tower? A stairway, spiral, a round window. He's surprised to discover himself here, not entirely displeased. The air smells wooingly. He's at the window. In view, the greensward, hare playing there. He stands to attention, spectator. Hare alerts, juicy leveret, randy in the eye, hears someone watching. 'What is it, ' I nudge, 'about the hare?' 'The moon?' he wonders. B plus. Hare scarpers. Goat in its place. Kid-goat. 'Used to sell them in Moore Street,' he responds, 'O Hanlon's, skinned, ready to roast.' 'Indulge?' 'No.' Flesh-eater – but picky. Try boar. He was brought up in *Coill an Chollaigh*, The Wood of the Boar, there has to be a gap, a cat-flap, a slit, a slot, who bent the coin that it stuck, Buddy? We meet a boar, young, amiable – as boars go, this pair could get on – but on what terms? He ate wild boar, yes, in Italy, once, salty beyond the palatable, slugging flagons since to staunch the parch. But this young boar, hairy Ben Bulben model, love that tusk, it wants you! And we both draw attention to an unusual feature, *specialité du jour*, could be, I'd say Yes, good bet, unusual feature, our eyes light on boar's left foot, there's a claw or talon or hook, hook it is, sprouting from that left foot, backward sprout, come-an'-get, spiked cocktail, open bar. 'What's he up to with that hook?' Fret, trickle of, in the interrogation. The boar, grunty, measures the questioner for size. 'What's anybody up to with a hook?' Boar's away, hook shining. An agreed corrosive silence. Move to lower temperatures, cold-blooded creatures, turn on the heat. A shore – where The Armada shivered, left an anchor, barnacled *bon voyage*. A snake, raw umber, bottle green, lozengy pattern, wreathes the anchor's upright, twirls and turns – how emblematic can you get! Still, take or leave … Gottfried Benan Gauleiter Thinlip takes a load of it. Watch this, extends a foot. To play with – no, to steady – firm! The snake in its recreation. Snake goes still. The foot is removed. 'Thoughts on the snake?' 'The Other, forever Other.' Surprise you sometimes, he would. Later that evening, and I'm watching him over a book, a picture. A tiny deer, slick from the hind, furls from the mouth of a challengingly small pipe. Breathes the world. Unto us a ...? A pause? Velleity? Nostrum? 'Monaghanoose,' I hear beside me, 'The Hiding-Place of the Deer.'

In Loco Parentis

The father would station himself at the living-room front window, pocket his fists, examine the maieutic trees. What he was thinking about wasn't easy to know, his facts, fancies – this is not to say that he was inscrutable. Never that. Look at him and you'd say – 'There's a man who has right respect for rain' – and you'd be correct, he always carried an umbrella, black, sunniest day of the year he would not go forth without that umbrella. A man, then, who took rain seriously – but had enough texture to suffer contradiction; he sang when required, had been in his youth, and past youth, a rubicund tenor, *Pinafore* and *Ruddigore* in the upstairs of the old Market House, pooch and you might well find a warm tuning-fork on his person. Respected rain. Sang. Also, a penitent something, truthfully, filming the mouth. Smoker – when The Five Continents smoked – he'd given up on tobacco, as sacrifice, offering in pursuit of a Special Intention: yet here too, happily, contradiction. Non-smoker, he allowed himself a few cigarettes a day, they were never lit, his lips played, rolled them, back and forth, diligently released strands of tobacco, with like diligence – tongue assisting lips assisting teeth – collected, kneaded, these to a unity, discarded, after an hour or so, the moist detritus.

His hair. It – most of all – requested commentary. An Old Trouper white, and – possibly – once permed, measured curls there in an obstinate vein that didn't suggest nature's bestowal. You wouldn't enquire. Nor would you concerning the remarkable blanch. It was said that the hair turned overnight, result of a boating accident on the lake. He'd been oaring for Dockery, the draper – who had a mania for shooting pike, April, as they rose for the spawning – and he couldn't have luck. A boar-pike attacked the boat – or it hit a submerged log – accounts varied. The boat capsized, Dockery drowned, survivor oarsman's hair next morning this Christmas crown. Again a contradiction – the father still rejoiced in pike from the lake. Never set foot in a boat from that evening but – hot from the pan, bread-crumb batter, a pike's a feed. Mind the bones.

Love – or the rumours of love – came into that business also. Dockery – as it happened, and it would happen – was an 'admirer' of the woman the father would one day marry, and, rambunctious spirit, fancied his prospects. This is mentioned because it's true, inveigles. If all the lakes were inhabited and melic, as they audibly were, they were all – abundantly – love-stories. That lone angler, years dead, still to be seen fishing on summer evenings, had, in his fifties, fallen for a local *seod* who hadn't yet seen twenty-one. She may have encouraged him, he was well-to-do, a fair catch. Next, to the equable surprise of all – equable because, it had to be admitted, her action was bizarrely in fashion – she dropped everything to become a nun, Missionary Order, vanished into the Punjab, never to be seen again this side of the world. A month later, her suitor committed himself to the waters in quiet of October dusk.

The mother, by the way, had a love-story, and a shooting, to match the best in a highly emulous field. She was in her final year with the Louis nuns in Carrick, and great with Mark Clinton, Mark, second-cousin once removed, charmer, rising football star, and (as his sister sang) 'Torso from the Greeks'. A land ruction spouts, Clintons in the thick of it when they'd be a sight better off minding the forty acres of stoney *clábar* they tilled. Mark, Monday morning, went to the field of quarrel, yoked the horses, commenced to plough. He lasted ten yards, sniper took him out, first the horses, then Mark, middle of the forehead. He'd written his love-letter on the Saturday, Headmistress handed it to the addressee early on the Monday – sniper, could be, just snuggling himself into position. Talk of the dispute, the letter carried, and the words – 'Likely I'll be all right but, if I'm not, shure you'll come – the girl in the song – and weep over my grave.'

That was all in another time – yet never far away. The mother would stare the window, study the round of the lawn, and it was easy to know what she was thinking, the tone if not the precise topic. Her expression conveyed a full measure of suspicion across a broad sweep, that tranche given substance by an inimitable *Hmmm* – lugubrious, questing, finally summarizing verdict from between closed lips and pale. A woman who didn't say much – yet you'd never call her taciturn. She wrote letters ceaselessly, more letters than anyone on earth. To everyone. About everything. Nothing. And, it followed, received letters by the sackful, handbag always swollen with mail incoming, outgoing, some arcane filing-system in her fingertips that worked, and – watch her hands move among those sheaves – lent her disordered pleasure. As did, it's worth noting, quotations from the great – The Bard, Burns, Mangan, Tennyson – which laced her correspondence. Favourite quotation, while we're on the topic – *You see me, Lord Bassanio, where I stand.* Runner-up – *She should have died hereafter.* Third place – *My salad days, when I was green in judgment …*

Give him a word – *austere*. Give her a word – *constraint*. She might, once upon a time, have permitted herself a drop of Winter's Tale but not now with years. She had put aside alcohol (so, indeed, had the father) as sacrifice, offering in pursuit of a Special Intention. Withdrawal there, and she had, was, withdrawn but, beware of liberties, stayed in charge. Younger, much, than the father – he was, more, grandfather to the house – she would sit on his knee when there was company, flirt prettily with him, exhibit her winding little finger in its casual conquering mode. Guests, audience, departed, she'd revert, offer you again boxed novice, nun, busy Reverend Mother logging distress signals that, studied, slowed her step. Quickened and slowed.

If she had a single extravagance, it was, not improbably, hats. Miss Mc Donagh, who taught in the Girls' National, went to London every summer for a week, and, under instructions, returned with a selection of hats, the boldest colours, shapes and shimmers, hats veiled, feathered, sequined, hats for a wedding, a christening, day at the zoo, hats for Corpus Christi, the Assumption, hats for Our Lady of Knock. Transformer hats! She became her forgotten opposite, flashed flapper glances, wore six different creations the one jocund day, you'd fall in love with her again, the father – leaning on his umbrella, did, unbeknownst to himself. Under the carousel sign of the hats, she won a hundred pounds in the Sunday Crossword, took the bus to Dublin, came home with more hats, the autumn range, it was a madness – in vermilion, mauve, cardinal red, cerise, it was her – or a bit of her, people smiled, vouchsafed her entitlement, muttered good-luck to the fling, poor creature had her own troubles, God help her.

Troubles. *Never trouble trouble till trouble troubles you* – but the sampler had no admonition on the next move, grief wasn't in its repertoire. Grief, sing or cry it, united the father and mother, ancestral grief, immediate sitting-at-the-table grief, adulterated cosmic grief. And there was at least one other symbiotic bond. A genuflectory tic. Acknowledge this as endemic but, in justice, concede the rider: they were exemplary. Annually, they'd wait – eyes out on poles – for what were known as *The Changes*, meaning the movement of priests from parish to parish, promotions, sideways shifts, reprimands overt and disguised. Promotions were, properly, the focus, the nub. On hearing that Father So-and-So had been advanced to Parish Priest of Such-and-Such, their mutual joy was to perform while others were still assimilating the news. Hire a taxi. An expense – but justifiable. Make the journey, knock on that varnished door, enter, and, humbly proud, utter congratulations, shape obeisance generally to the theme of the hour. It needn't take long, home James (from the promoted one, pasha wave at the window) in swelters of satisfaction that would bandage for a month and a day.

Think of ghosts, timid in their trappings, ghosts en route to being authorized spirits. They would hear – she, in particular could hear – noises in the trees and stippling between-light that might have clarified much but remained moored just beyond the intelligible. She, it goes (almost) without saying, was a haunted ghost, he a ghost stopped in time and space and random event. They looked at the boy, and the father, deferential, left it to her. She knew the boy to be something she had chosen not to be, a living danger, and, to herself, had no hesitation in saying so. The girl was another matter. While the father stood firm by the window, counting the trees, the mother, again, took the fragile initiative, brooded on the girl, girl now and in time to be. Something had happened. A fault. Carelessness. *Given*, you could now call it a given. Where would it conclude? On whose doorstep and in what purgatory clime? These were questions for tomorrow and tomorrow out to the last syllable creeping in its petty pace, English her best subject bar one, Religious Knowledge, there she topped the class, deckled certificate still hanging above her bed to state, authenticate, *sotto voce* preserve that achievement against the weight, mordant, of seasons, grasping cycles of the moon.

A Tree, a Shell

The ash with mossed treasure flourished. A freckener, was, is, will forever be, bleed you to see the shellfish surface from butt of the ash – such softly rounded thunder, how did the tree stay in one piece? Stayed in one piece because large bivalve and tree were in league, were one, about the same business under the star-wheel, whatever that odd business might be. The shell, handsome cobalt blue, arranging itself in a central cleft, was openly on display – do come and window-shop, closer, come closer – while retaining all the time, and as much displaying, a tough calculating knowledge of the pinioned scrutineer, boy-traveller, hello out there, news is you're going to have to talk to me, touch me, eat me, and I taste so venally of – *us both*, that's what bugs you, you're so tenterhooks – didn't you ever before see an honest shellfish rejoice in itself, open-a-bit, shut-a-bit, one-steps, two-steps, divil knows what new steps – are shells not per-mitted to shake-a-leg – and then, timing – o, exquisite, open that little bit more – reveal my entire belongings, the pink-flesh, bud of, deliquescent, pulsing, I want *out*, I want conversation, I too have my ownsome lonesomes, want to talk to you, lip you, guz-zle your sweetmeats– you're so mealy-mousey, little-does-your-mother-know-you're-out – shout for peripheral Daddy – call Calico Tom – the girl? She won't help you. Tell you change your nappy. PS: I won't go away, you know.

The ash with mossed treasure flourished knob, fold, cleft, flourished May Herrity, an Indian maiden, at twelve tall beyond understanding, gait of the select, and darkly lacquered hair to the meandering small of her back. More remarkable, however, than anything in the ring of works and days, was her complexion, colouring fore and aft, amber enjoying an umbra of gold, she was the Indian gipsy maiden, with remove to match, consciousness of her status that perfumed streets, doorways, untidy slopes of sleep and waking. This must be what they called *style*. Knowing, to the last ounce, her value, knowing the homage she commanded, she – thoughtlessly – established, and kept, a distance, thus enhancing value and respect, enhancing the ground she trod. She knew all she needed to know. If you'd find her now, seek, pilgrim, somewhere in heights of the ash where she is (undoubtedly) sunning herself on a weightless and invisible landing, plinth awarded her by air, water, the giving hand of the hills, to further inclination, destiny, her immutable ranking above the fray.

She never spoke – or she was never known to speak. That fitted beautifully, there could be no argument. What was there for her to say – that was not already said? Her conversation moved so eloquently on a variety of topics, there was little she – little anyone – could possibly add. Yet it pleased us to imagine that she spoke – that she would speak – to us, one of us, some of us … What that voice would resemble, what would she say … Would she – could she – might she – but imagination recoiled, you couldn't venture into that bewitching problematic, it was presumptuous, flagrant – let it, simply, be. What this supernal creature said, she – silently – said. The question was, rather: can you – your dishcloth ears – hear the secrets she, so plentifully, disburses and withholds?

Binkie Mc Elroy spoke. It was constant amazement what girls did with their voices – kept them penned – or freed them – on a leash – off the leash – never sign of a leash – a bit of the road with everyone. Binkie's voice was ever cursive, musked, broderie: lean towards her to hear, you needn't, not really, but that invitation was in the pitch of her call, her presence, and you responded.

You responded – without listening for meaning, for meaning didn't (in the normal sense) interest you, didn't interest her, music was the concern, her music-room, sanctum where she lived, moved, held her being, and to which you, fortunate one, have just been invited. Safe landing!

The room was blonde, yellow curtains everywhere, it was morning and sunlight was pouring through the balmy windows and promised to – swore to – continue that munificence while time endured – and beyond. A blonde room, a-tisket, a-tasket, a green and yellow basket. The room was a basket, lightly uphol-stered, nothing fulsome, the note was so – throwaway, not quite throwaway, just stopped the temptress side of throwaway. Binkie was everywhere in the room. She offered fruit that 'just happened' to be handy – cherries, wild damsons, strawberries – 'Strawberries and cream? Strawberries need cream?' Figs – yes – for the associations, dates – for the stickiness. She'd take you to the one picture in sight, picture of a cat, proudly yellow, with a green, translucent green, frog perched on its back. 'A gift', she'd say, 'from a dear friend. Call it my signpost picture.' And she'd fling herself on a convenient couch.

This was not comether, the room, in fact, was ante-room – it took shape as she sat up, she carried it with her, waved it about. Her real room was, naturally, in the inexhaustible summer of that laden tree, same floor as May Herrity's but opposite wing, find her, any morning you like, up there, shaking the leaves, strutting her wares, Binkie's the fair tomboy lure, she knows nothing of the word *remove*, she's conversable, forward, *gamine*, floats from ash to The Bathing Hole – we have now reached her populist room – here there's sport among the minnows in the brown-and-yellow swirl, and, liquid medallion, Binkie astride or spreadeagled upon the anointed backs of favoured dolphins, tossing smiles to the starved queue moored on the bank, gawky in the seething water, her quick arms, legs' candescence, calling the tune, nobody paid the piper, piper was manifold, ubiquitous, sun on the sluggish river, whimsies in the breath, migrant thigh, minnows who knew the whole story and frisked omniscience, listen, listen to the Binkie song, her daily composition, gift for you if you've hands to play, dice to fling, I am the Gulf Stream, she sings, damp of the morning, slick of noon, spill of dusk and charmed curvets of the midnight flow, if in the stunned blue of my Empress eyes you see – folding past, present, and ineluctable to come – lips of the bivalve open and shut, open again, hear squeeze-box in the cleft release a hoyden chord to toast the ribs, why then, sign on, faint, expire, dismember, you've flown this hour the golden mile ...

Kitty Mc Carron shouted, never spoke – that would have abjured her nature. All the Mc Carrons shouted, everything they possessed gave raucous support, radios, gramophone, alarmclocks, whetstone, breaking delph, an off-key cornet, hammers, tongs, hatchets, that small house fronting the street was the font of uproar, mother, father, sons, daughters, engendered din – that was their way, yours to live with, and, of a piece, the daughters teemed children, the children added to the uproar, and promised – soon as sky gave leave – to toss more shouters into the fray. Bedlam be thy sword. The din – seldom if ever harmonious – still had some hale quality that curbed protestation. Pride in Bedlam might have been it. It was as if the Mc Carrons, idler life giving them leave to probe the tyrant question of occupation, had sensed a corner that might be theirs, stepped forward, hollering, and found a cause.

Kitty Mc Carron, buxom Kitty from the far side of the tracks, blest Bedlam her cradle and inheritance, mother a notorious barge, father ex-Merchant Navy, tattooed to prove it, all the Mc Carrons were tattooed, Kitty was tattooed – where the boy feared to tread, perchance to dream, his fear her wand, inked needle, and serpent's tail. When, full-buttocked, she shifted a generous cheek on the street windowsill she honoured, love-ditties banned by Church and State issued from her creases, enough to quench reason, liberate in the down-draught snouty treble of pigs at feeding-time and ne'er a pig in sight, shiver for your bacon, childybawn, let custody of the eyes shutter you from her transmitter wardrobe (will it?), wispy glad rags that know her unassuageable appetites, proclaim temporary arrangement, clasp-and-button mere happenstance, caprice of the breeze: she wears – herself, red-head, by decree – compels all candidates for subjugation to honey-finger her furbelow tattoo, surrender free-will and all its tiresome pomps, done, switch of her tail, she's up and away, leads all her pigs to market, just a ruse, she has other plans, her small loud eyes dart with plans, she whines, snorts, the boy grunts – was that a grunt, little does-mammy-know-you're-out – truffles for tea? – Kitty has troughs for the fat, troughs for the lean, she whinnies east and she bugles west, heads her every last *banbh* back to that complicitous ash and up into those foddered parlours, salaaming, trotter to forehead, rump to the floor, as she passes the sacral bivalve, salute for the flutter, pink-flesh, fateful maw that would not, could not, now be stayed.

Out hunting all day, no game. It grew dark on the mountain, cue the fog, indeterminate, strict. He lost his way, whizz in the head, no footing bar the stray sod. He sat down on a rock. After a while, window opens in the fog. He saw a house, white-washed, solid two-storey, hello in the dusk, promise of food and shelter. Make for that house.

He knocked on the door, opened it. Bare enough kitchen. No occupants bar an old man lying by the fire and a bullocky sheep by the far wall. He went in and sat down. The old man looked up. 'You're welcome.' 'Was I expected?' Something in the voice. 'Who's unexpected?' Warrior began to have his doubts. A roof. That itself. But food? Drink? Company? He sat there, saw a tuft of flour on the table try to shape itself into a tiny stag. No go. Tuft of flour. As you are.

After a while the old man stirred his rump – there was someone else in the house, turned out. He called loudly – 'Come, will ye.' A young woman appeared from a room behind the kitchen. 'Give him a bite.' The young woman, able as well as beautiful, readied food and drink, set everything on a table, departed the kitchen. Warrior sat down to eat. As he took his first taste, the sheep along the wall broke her tether, rushed the table, knocked it over, scattered the meal, all directions. 'She's rowdy habits,' the old man allowed. 'Tie her up.'

Warrior rose, caught the sheep by the head and tried to drag her to the wall. She resisted. He fought her and lost. 'Can't tie a bit of a sheep with a bit of a rope,' says the old man. He himself would do it. He rose, wobbled from the hearth, ashes streaming – tidal – from the britches. He took the sheep by the scruff, at his ease pulled her to the wall, tied her up, returned to his nest by the fire.

Quiet. Creaky. Food and drink on the floor. 'Give him something to eat,' the old man called again to the young woman. She appeared, went to work, again put food and drink before the Warrior. She left the kitchen. 'Mangey boovey,' the old man said. Warrior ate and drank, meal for a prince. He moved back from the table, rested a minute, fixed his eyes on the room where he knew the young woman to be. You must speak to her.

He went down to the room, there she was, brimful of the journey that was hers. She looked at Warrior, the look contained him. She spoke – 'You had me once. You won't have me again.' He mightn't know much but he knew dismissal. Spit curdled, he turned, humped back to his chair in the kitchen. The sheep looked at him, disinterestedly. The old man slept in the ashes. What time was it of day or night? The young woman came into the kitchen.

'You're wondering,' she said. 'You weren't lost by accident. Why were you lost? Find out. That sheep isn't of the usual kind. She is Strength. The old fella in the ashes is Death. Me? You had me before, you won't have me again. Still. Since you got this far, I'll give you whatever it is you ask for.' Warrior said nothing. 'Why don't you speak?' 'I don't know.' 'Well, I know. So you might as well speak.' Hazel eyes in her head shone like the wave. 'I'd rather go now.' 'To be sure. The kind you are'd rather go. Try to go, why don't you?' Her right hand was sainted song – you'd howl for its ease – but he could catch in it, refined as it was, might of an army. 'Give over the palaver, will you?' the old man growled from the ashes. The young woman sat down, stretched her shanks like a runner, race over or about to commence. No clock ticked. It was a quarter-past nine, not a wrinkle, and time slowing up. Warrior spoke. 'Listen. I sinned once with the beautiful dead. Take from me this smell of clay.' He's alone again on the mountain.

No date ...

With Sam the Man this time, the baby-blue Protestant eyes remotely evangelical, we're at Ardlow, Place of the High Lake, mother-country for country matters. The hill behind the hayshed – you could sing it. Portora arises. 'You should have thieved Joyce's *Place-Names* from the Library that winter evening you had the chance. Never fingered, as you noticed, never, never. Ulster will. *Toujours*. Volume might've learned you something. Might, I say.'

Always regretted that missed thievery by the winding banks of Erne, Sam's cool – 'Why don't you hit someone your own size?' – whauping along the silent corridors. Where were they all? Christmas vacation, now you remember. Carry on, Portora! He's pointing out mushrooms, buttony, which I pick. We come on some more parasoly, with a red tinge, detonations, here's metal more attractive. He glosses – 'Agaric. Female cathartic, male tinder.' I pick some, discard them behind his sacristan back. 'Longevity', he says, Foxrock in the burr, 'is promised – if you're in the hunt for that. Certain natives – conceivably ours, crying in the rain – rub the drum with mushroom-ash to make it speak. *Secundum* The Hairy Fairy, The Immortals eat them together with cinnamon, gold and jade. *Cuisine minceur?* You pays your money.'

We part. Friends. He's started something. There's a pool of water in the Fort Field. There I find cavalier mushrooms thrusting for the surface, mouthing desire. I want them, their colours ignite me and I attend, you're talking claret, capucine, henna. Enter the pool. I'm in there – it's deep enough, my head on a level with the bank, smell danger, quagmirey underfoot. The mushrooms waiting for their Picasso, or Le Douanier, his Egyptian mode, the bank sprouts the boy, in his gob the sprig, cherry ripe.

She refers to 'the lustrous forms in their winter sleep'. What are my intentions? Honourable? Honorific? Froth? Cuckoo? Spit? We have too many who might know better 'lying on golden apples in the broken fields'. I could love – do – her articulation. Admire, better – she reads my qualifiers before I shape them. No let-up. You're on the hook. Some hook. Some opponent. 'Let's talk', she says, impish, 'of the *uber* in *exuberant*.' Looks through me and that look's chop sui generous. To go no further. Christ spare me the RLS denouement. And Babel, spectacles on nose and autumn in his heart, calling from the gates – 'I was not given time to finish.'

Filmic, isn't it? I suppose. Reredos? (Post-card: 'At the Rats' Wedding a little mouse came out to play.')

Date indecipherable ...

The window was closed. The window's open. *Pro tem*. We converse through an open window. Airily washing dishes, I look at her. Frank. I want to be frank. *Sans ambages*. I am. Within the conventions – 'Perhaps we should talk?' 'You mean' – tender / implacable the gaze – 'move the furniture around?' I sometimes ponder where we'll stop. Will she evaporate? Petrify me? 'No – I would like to talk.' 'Know your ambition?' 'I have ambition?' 'Your desire is to be the Pillar-Monk, the Stylite, up there solipsizing away to yourself, Perpetual Night of the Big Wind.' A draughty leave-taking.

1 January 1990

O, Hyacinthus Celticus mine, recite *mensa, mensa, mensam, amo, amas, amat,* I'm dirt, you the brush, what you keep forgetting is that I was with you that night on the narrow road which leads to the bothawn on the mother's side – country matters, *mon cher*, I was the moon that blanched your smig, full moon of May (Our Lady's month!), note precise position chosen for the combat on that (Famine) road – right by the stile – that Mary sat on, yes, before she got the stool, stiles, turnstiles, posterns, gates give off music of the *main-à-main* had we the ears to catch it – bright and brighter that dirt ribbon, rip of *timor mortis* through you, audible, this degree of illumination is five degrees below zero, it has such intent, rattled the whites of your eyes, high noon for the Warrior bold, his hayro-halo missing in action or not yet, possibly, forged, world's gone pale, drained to the lees, you're alone bar the dog and my moon-eye, wattage rocketing, and here she comes, sashaying towards you – is she weasel, stoat or mutant mink or is she Mae West come east, That a banana in yer pants or you juz glad to see me? It's stoat, Mistress Stoat – the word of 'unknown origin' – 'the European ermine, especially in her brown summer coat' – she's a beaut, those pikey teeth, and how she waltzes with hot eyes for you, The Man in the Gap, teasing her power, testing her power like an *ingénue*, her milky wiles, she comes close and closer – syrup at the knees, aren't you? – I know, I know, she does that to everyone she crosses – now she sways, shadow-sway (that fulgid moon, don't forget, remember The Porter!) beside her, and look, between her and the grass verge, a hand – whose? – lying there, spilling dust and ashes, there should be a law against that but Dame Stoat's law is Kingdom of Kerry law – 'to do no right and brook no wrong', are you okay? – don't be afraid to sweat, healthy habit – tell her to leave if you don't fancy the gig, get the hell outa here in her summer coat and whiskers *en garde*, look at the bitch now, she poses like a model, displays teeth (again) and rump, does her belly-dance, sumptuary, Nureyev, here's your Princess, in heat, she is molten, mate, – where's your dog – you had a dog, didn't you? – now I remember, dog fled, the friend of man knows when to scram, he has good teachers, *flip*, stoat reduced to – she really is a class act – reduced, simply, Ripley, to black believe-it-or-not tail of winter, upright brush grinning questions from her endless store, brash besom – good nine inches – cavorts in your shadow – now do not faint, don't, spoil everything – she much prefers to hypnotize her subject – what's that sound? – black besom's tongue, is it, lisping love-song, no words, sinuate zone of the sub-verbal that sticks to the sweat-spots, pussy tail breathes you, takes your sniff-print, your spoor – why don't you engage her? She's lonesome in her own mountebank way, no matter, delighted, the hoor, to have your spoor – you never knew you had a spoor among your bric-à-brac, lots forget they have a spoor – Christ, she's gone, would you credit it, made her impression – took yours – and gone – call for your dog – find your voice – shout for the dog, man – *come back to what's left of you, child* – can it be, looks like it is, first time you've known such ruckled fear under the moon, lovely night if you're up for it, heavy fall of dew – look at the shine of your boots – mushrooms the morra, a black hare – she's carrying a secret that lass – lopes past, say Hi, hoppity-hippety, entirely self-possessed, truth of animals chiming in that nocturne noggin – well, it's grand to see you in the raw, damp forehead, shoulders mauled, respiration shallow, nearly – I should say it – handsome, unimaginable

how much more textured the beast is when he's not onstage, true
what they say, the scholarship of man's a kind of rape ...

Months later ...
'Your patience.' 'What about it?' 'It amazes.' 'Don't push it, friend,
you've seen it crinkle. Remember the night you supplied me with
crutches – your totem furniture! – hand-made, State of the Art,
such veneer, such dedication, the devotee in you, all those prayers
and hymns obeisant and crawthump litanies over the centuries, o,
blood, blood has mountains, you recorded – I trust – the crutches'
thunder as they bit the floor – and I put the question – 'Aren't you
open to the fear of calamity?' – and I can, as can you, recall the
ditty troglodytic in reply – 'No, not in this instance, anyway.' That
was a close-run thing, *a stór*, my hand was on the button, kettle-
drum of the crutches' tarrantara reaming your resistant duodenum,
you awoke, heart yammering, and, callow pedagogue, *habitué* of
The Blue Angel, Emil Jannings you never lost it, felt for the first
time since when – since Mistress Stoat? – your doors fly open to
the fear of calamity.

'Why bother?' 'I'm appointed. I attend. I meet circumstance, respond. Accordingly. You're an experiment. So am I – come to think
of it.' 'Is Tolerance your name?' No instrument in sight, she aus-
cultates me. 'Ever hear the story of the man who developed a fix-
ation on dear Old Lilith? He decides he must – somehow or other
– it's a compulsion – it's fate – it's curiosity – it's who won the
match? – he must find her, wherever she is, say Hi. An admirable
explorer, a Scott, a Shackleton, more Shackleton than Scott, blad-
dery eye of the wayward Celt, musically given, string section, clit
for preference, he travels land and sea, roll-call of years, patience
undimmed, and, with the help of The Powers (watching over him,
Satellite, ley-lines, digital dithyrambic, whole works) doesn't he
eventually catch up with her, middle of nowhere, that's Lilith, Our
Bearded Lady, Cinque, Rue Vitale, up there in the 16th, yes, there
she is looking out the window, never sleeps, case she'd miss some-

thing, you know the women, so, she waves, 'Come on in.' In he goes, bursting out all over, *en fleur, en châleur*. She embraces him – she's so feely-uppy Madame Lilith – Irish genes there somewhere, I'd swear, check it out sometime – she embraces him, '*Mon Petit!*' And – one bite – whips his head off. Tusitala, teller of tales, called it a 'convulsion in nature' – last words, you'll remember, in the novel unfinished, call it anything you like, my grandmother called it 'The Price'. You've heard of The Price? 'O, yes.'

She is what I require. To a certain degree. Only. Also: to a limitless.

Call It a Nest

The Workhouse was itself in all lights, in no light. Morning, it would not be beguiled – speak of August morning beguilement – no, it remained the potent keep, gapped container, that cupped all recipes, no placebos. Noon and it took what came – it knew what was to come, noon did nothing for it, one way or another, let Angelus beat in vain against its smokeless chimneys – *Laud ye the Gods* – it had heard one Angelus too many, temple clapper, muezzin howl, distractions for the gullible it could do without but, if the gullible needed such, then let them suck Koranical bullseyes till the cows came home, ruminate, masticate, regurgitate certificates of proud standing, it had its own Stoneybatter nourishment, it believed in its own One, Holy, and Despotic Church, and the name of that church was writ in Stone, cannibal immemorial Stone; dusk it came into its own, flowered stone, brimmed worshippers, disowned them in a twinkle, called them again, distributed petrified wafers to a cowering fold, shut shop. Night. Don't enquire of its night devotions.

Restless from ward to ward, odd jackdaw for company, the boy toured the ruin. Air hung heavy, smell of rot, a stew of molasses. He'd tried a handkerchief mask and it had brought relief, briefly, then became clogged with the worst he met, and he pitched it aside. You must breathe the joint, the joists, the grooves. He'd no idea what hour of bell or clock it might be, the light no clue, it was dream-light, enough to show him what he was intended to see, didn't utter beyond that. He roamed permissive acres. Size of the wards, swollen lath-and-plaster, stone stairways without beginning, without end, animal droppings – cats, dogs, rats – frequent, withered, shrinking, freshly laid. He lost his bearings, almost his balance, as if some theft had left him light in the head, stopped, looked out a window. The Plantin', the lake. Not yet born, motionless. Blast of wind, and fragments of masonry, he guessed, whipped past, bounced hollowly on the field below, were still.

This place. *Where it commenced.* There was a confined, implacably locked, porch-cum-office jutting from the front of the building. *Admissions,* had to be. The couple of scrunched windows were blacked out. A door, sturdily hung, had that churchy air, forced respect, cried reprisal. The varnish on it had peeled to a yellow nothing with the years, and it followed the boy about, would-be familiar, invited him to linger in the cramped annex that was its pad and leprous chapel-of-ease. Stubbornly, he excused himself. The offer stood, trailed him with haughty nerve. *The finish of this place.* Right at the far back of the hulk, sucking the very foundations, was a kind of cellar. Push through singed scrub and fetid weed, you'd come to the mouth of a – hole, cave, cavern, burial-dump, it was whispered. Bodies dropped from a window convenient, thrown onto the barrows, no distance, chute them under. Inspect. Darkness. Glint of water. That depot, too, followed him about, breathy, and choking.

Where was he? Lumpy book on a window-ledge, book covered with dust. It met him with magistral clout, whatever it harboured, and he was not about to probe. Touch it. His hand was water. Move on, leave it – but he couldn't. Yet. Now from the ragged spine a bevy of pismires, willowy extended family, raced, slicked-up for the outing, disappeared into neighbouring grime. You can move. By no means. From the inhabited spine this time the snout of a brazen mouse – or a young rat, pair of eyes, nail-head, that struck him. Vanished. Get out of here. He made for a doorway, on the way out was directed to look back. No book on the ledge. In its place a listless nettle growing, black butterfly settled on its tip. Eyes glued, he willed that butterfly to move, lift, fly. Not a tremble. Listless nettle. Black butterfly, inert, on the tip. Sheen of that black.

He took the stairs down to the next floor, halfway down got stuck, his feet wouldn't free themselves from the clingy stone. He tugged, dragged, he clawed. Useless. Stand still. Listen, he thought, or prayed. So he listened. Nothing. Listened on. After a minute, less, came a huge churn of steps – every conceivable beat, light, heavy, young, old, firm, slithery, the lost, the found. Without protest, he let the steps enter his feet, rise and travel inside him. For a moment, he was a busy procession, amiably keyed, liberating; his bones, cavities, accepted the feckless gatherum of the invasion, he was free again to move, and did, the steps departing him simultaenously, unhurried, off to their next assignment.

Another ward, the same, they were all the much of a muchness. *Welcome* – some recent hand had chalked in mauve on the floor. A pigeon rummaging a pile of rubble, jerked, took off, bisected a window, no more. At the far end of the ward, easy in a doorway, he saw the girl. Sitting on a swing – he recognized the lawn swing, it swayed – slowly, untroubled, he could hear the ropes' submissive creak against the seat's timber. The girl was dressed in white, and wearing a pink bonnet. 'How d'ye like me Easter bonnet?' The word *bonnet* – she made it to soar, dance heights of the ward like a kite in the full of its health, tugged a cord and yanked it this way and that against the chaos of rotten ceiling, cobwebs from the year before cobwebs were spun, she crowed – 'All the ribbons on it!' 'Melodious,' he answered. She smiled, wasn't there any more, unvisibled.

But leaving the silver fox in her stead. He knew this fox, couldn't say from where the first day, but knew him well as bread. Ask anyway. 'Where're you from?' 'All over.' 'Do I look like a *clob*?' 'Mandalay.' 'Where's that?' 'The sun comes up like thunder.' 'Where's Mandalay?' 'China across the bay.' The fox didn't look the least Chinese. On second thoughts, he did, far more Chinese than lots you'd see in the papers or at the pictures. Comical gaze through the ambush eyes that first meeting – as right this minute. 'Hello.' Open-air voice. The fox came towards him, friendly as usual, knocked him down, this was their ritual, they wrestled in the dust, play-acted. Every so often, the fox would go still, just stand there, this was the boy's chance to study. *An sionnach geal* – the bright fox, not many around, and those in it seldom seen. This pelt, coronal, was from somewhere apart, whorled an unwritten weather. That eye, guide in the pupi, had met musicians on the way, a damp nose milked the breeze. 'Lick me,' the boy requested.

This was the cure for what ailed – anyone. Not quite. The fox – you could tell – did not dispense favours indiscriminately, picked his patients, the boy, eager, from first glimpse, to be among them, and knowing, from a passing cloud, the application to lie in the tongue. So. 'Lick me.' And it had happened, was happening. Underdown light in the tongue, fox licked his face and head, eyes, ears, mouth, nose, throat. There was a method to the licking that the boy could never quite make out, perhaps a method that altered every time while becoming still more method, some essential replication visible – and out of sight, as juices, salve, salvo, *Salve, Regina*, opened the pores, simpled the blood, altered the face of things in a way you could only describe by keeping it to yourself – or conveying with a glance – that defied description. The pair of them now lay still, his head resting on the fox's shoulder. Free as a bird, he slept.

And awoke. Smell of the fox, ditches, earth, gorse-blossom, beside him. Same fox, different coat, hooped black-and-green, me bucko had Bamboozalem for tailor. The fox frowned. 'Jemmy Cullen shouldn't sell that horse.' 'I'll tell him.' Next topic. The fox led him from that dungeon as if he knew it inside out and took him a short distance across the fields in the direction of The Plantin'. Bye-bye tumble in the grass, *slán beo* lick on the cheek, the boy alone. On a path to The Plantin'. He scouted. Blue-grass. The whins. Bog-myrtle to deck the bride. On the path, not far ahead, he spots an egg, full of your hand – that size egg, half-hidden in the grass, shifting in its form – hare disturbed. He attended. Moved closer. The egg, hurrying, took off down the path to The Plantin'.

The boy stood where he was. Wobbled on his pins. Shook himself, set out after the egg, at a run, barely able to keep up. Consistently, the egg would melt into scutch-grass but he managed to track it, came to an understanding: the egg was teasing him, needling, playing him, the egg wanted him, could be – was – on his side. What side was that? They were approaching The Plantin'. The egg shot into it. The boy pursued. The Plantin' – fir dominant, the noble fir – was more welcoming than he'd anticipated, not hostile, at any rate. Awake, say. Ten yards into it, he came on the egg. A hut met him, ramshackle, shabby. He went to the door, such as it was, aperture, put his head in. Hovel, if ever you live to meet one. In a corner, small pile of old sticks, scantling or two. Nest. Sortov. Streaked with blood and dirt, the egg was sitting there. The egg stared him.

Upstairs in the Tent

First time he'd taken her there, he and the girl went to visit the grandmother in the tree. Sharp drying day but shelter among the leaves. They found the grandmother smoothing the idol lightly with the amber ball of her thumb. 'This blaycher's in no great hurry,' she reported, 'but he'll rouse yet and he'll warble.' 'What'll he warble?' – the girl. 'Not the Flash but the Flow, jig past forgetting mostly forgotten, know it?' She fetched the girl's hand, rested it on the emerging head – and, opinion of the boy, the head responded but he could have been making it up – 'You'll depart imaginin' you're just arriving,' Old Master Trainor epitaph'd him. The girl strayed her hand about the timber – pianist *pianissimo*, imp'd with her own thoughts, among those daffodils let the hare sit.

That was fine (not to boast of it). The three of them settled on a fork, traffic-island, of the southward-singing limb, and the grandmother took hold of the girl's face, avid fingers touring nose, cheek-bones, forehead, informed blind reading from the dotted page. She spent a long day with the pearl-tinted eyes that sopped green of the tree. 'Where'd you get those eyes?' 'I've only the loan of them.' 'From?' Kept mum. 'Windgall and waterfall, would it be?' 'Could occur', the girl steadied herself, 'an' never happen.' Another of her stock phrases. 'Windgall's the sign of storm, and waterfall – depends how you sip it,' the grandmother drooped her eyelids, raised them slowly. 'Then you could say that about lots – frogs red in the fields, foam on the rock, say.

You've a vessel in your ear for the music, bestowed thing, always a charge for that. What age would you be?' 'Five – I believe.' 'A good age. As these things go.'

Shot off a shovel, a pigeon broke from the tree. The boy startled, signature sound, contestant self-propelled into worlds of possibility. The bole, hospitable, soaked the racket, tucked it away. Beyond the chapel, Kangley's jackass sobbed from the groin – 'Mr *Crescendo*,' the grandmother jeered – foosthered with pedals and stops, wheezed to an empty meeting-house. They heard the front gate open and shut. 'What's that for?' The girl pointed to the trophy fingernail. 'Peel spuds next famine' – and, winking, hostess parts leaves to give them a window onto the avenue. A little old man – in from the hills by the step of him – into view, making for the house. (The hills gave a hoppity progress, and a tendency to shout – no one knew why – when talk would do.) The visitor was wearing a striking broad-brimmed hat, crown white, blue the band, black the brim. 'You'd thieve that lid,' the grandmother nodded salutations. 'Keep an eye on him now while he's in it.' Hoppity-hippety, the little old man kept going. Stopped. He'd felt their recording presence. Could be. But there was more, he'd work to do. Between lilac and roseydendron at a bend of the avenue, he was in partial shade from fir and yew – red of the yew-bark zinging of archers. Look at this now if ye're stuck for recreation. Even if ye're not. He took off the hat – gravely limber gesture, tossed it ahead of him. It soared ten yards, descended – as if lowered to the gravel by – birdsong, say. The old man fell to his knees. Bowed the head. Stooped and kissed the ground – the boy clutched the girl's hand, grandmother's arms steadied the two. Rising nimbly, powerful, old man on up the avenue, collecting his hat on the way, putting it on, slipping out of sight. 'Mind that,' the grandmother let the window swing *cogar-mogar* shut.

As the three swopped a look, exhilarated by bare simplicity of the action, she doled out nuts of some description. 'Down them.' 'What are they?' 'Pine. To firm the blood, anxious juice, the same blood.' 'Jemmy Cullen's giving me a white foal,' the girl plumped her feathers. 'The train-bearer I am.' 'More, more nor train-bearer', grandmother chewed, 'and made for a white foal, it'll arrive. Wouldn't like to light a match between ye. Jemmy *bocht*. Sold the horse, sold the harrow, crowbar's lying in a puddle by the back door. The men's the boys. Saw the father – grandpa? – I'd take my oath he whisked from child to grandpa – short-cuts for short rations – saw him busy the other day. Above the clock.' 'Windin' that clock,' chimed the girl. 'No daw this one,' the grandmother gave her another splash of the pine medicine. And described what she saw and they knew she saw, since they also had marked it for fevered and a burden. 'In with him to pounce on *The Occasion of Marriage* mantelpiece clock. He finds the key. Opens the glass front door. Brings the hands – ruler moving finger – to one o'clock. Lets the clock strike one. And he winds. And to two the hands. And strike. And he winds. And so around the dial – under the white head with the drownded air, that face of him like a wandering spade – around the dial, each hour visited, loosing the strike, and, after, the winding, tight and tighter moving of the hands, the striking, tight as the last hangman's noose the winding. Until he's through with it. And closes the glass front door. *Slap*. Pitches the key under the article where it simmers, hear it, odd times, near the boil. Turns his back, marches out and away. That's no way to wind a clock. Should be told – but then he knows, knew from knee-high. Ways of winding. That's not one of them.'

She pulled an earthenware jug from under her accoutrements, filled it with water from a basin of the tree, gave it to the girl and asked her to splash the idol. The girl, pleased, steadied herself, jug above the shaping head, humility of the same knob this minute, old traffic passing between it and the girl, the girl was keen to herself, thunder muted (even if you must listen to it), the girl poured, lisp of the water, sodden green-black the receiving brow. The Factory horn – put-upon, unconcerned – sang, dimmed into the faraway. The girl, hooked, arranged herself, poured again. Hoof-beats register, horse galloping the road, not usual that – bar you had bats' ears and there were those abroad who had, hoof-beats saying *Hello*, hoof-beats *Lead in your hams*, hoof-beats *Had your chance, missed it*. Girl croons. Grandmother gives permission for a third go. The girl poured, emptied the jug on the soaked aspirant. Listen. It came, an answering, hidalgo *grawg* of the heron disturbed – or elated – or the bit of both, that several times, coming straight at them, then, abrupt, shut-down. 'All kinds of ways o' sayin' hello,' the grandmother took back the jug. 'I've great time for the heron, watch him till moondown, quarehawk sippin' his shadow in the jiggety stream.'

The girl – something heard or fancied – opened another swaying window on the avenue. Comical old man was on his way back, business completed. A document signed. The father lent his bold signature, regularly, and for a puny fee, to documents signed in his witness. Comical old man halted, looked up, spotted the three on their perch. Recognition flowed betwen him and the grandmother, they could be brother and sister, husband, wife, they're gabbing, the boy read, only we're not allowed to hear. Agile on his own springy stage, the visitor about to perform again. Movements light as cannavaun: extended his right hand, palm upward (piebald palm), let them all drink that. Next, same dancer, grace in the move, he reversed the hand, palm downward now, motionless. Away with him, that's my caper for the day. He skipped on down the avenue, vanished from sight.

The boy practised the gesture, hand imitating it before he knew. Extended right hand, palm upward. Hould yer hoult. Reverse the hand, downward palm, still. 'Aye?' – the grandmother – 'What's that French for?' 'The hand knows.' 'Does it now?' 'It'll tell me.' 'If you keep it supplied – that's the hot number. *Rigor mortis* paw is a glut on the market. Off with ye now, I've to crank a few prayers.' They were on their way. '*Gearcaile*,' she called back the girl, kissed her behind the left ear, turned her upside down, bathed the girl's comfortable head in the leaves, leaves great with the girl, girl great with the leaves.

Drums

A seasoned silence, silence of the basin full, balanced. Emerge. Bawl. And be. Soon a hellion hullabaloo, in the hills drums loud and in the sourpuss towns, had been from God's old time, you could tell from the beat, these brawlers weren't blow-ins, shy novices, prentice fodder, they belonged, one with the intractable soil, Ice Age donation, that glitter sempitern, find it in packed blue of the eye, crisp lie of nimbus, halo's fulgence, and concur, they belonged, truly, knew their pedigree and muscled skills, they were Christ's drums beating the message, messages, amplification, exegesis, tireless in the van, sky-signs blossomed, gilded noticeboard, placard, megaphone, holy, masted, exorbitant, proclaimed – *This* way, *we* are The Word … Walk, brother, with *us, we* greet The One Risen – *Did you hear, child, what the man said?* – Shun heathen Gospel, honour in *our* gathering Light that Shineth – listen and thou shalt hear, listen in humble credence and hear and be saved, One with Him, in Bliss Perpetual, washed, swaddled, laid in downy beds of the blest, *One with Him* the martyred drums pounded and – thrice-tested in the fire – the flounced bells pealed, brass bands rose out of insidious night, shimmered, gave tongue, and were gone to their next urgent summons, gone to hail – or loose precursor harmonies for – the striding preachers, tight-necked, blood-pressure jowls and lantern-jaws, trusty in pulpit or on tub, steps, cart or cobbled market-square, great names among them, Bishop Bailie, Pastor Mc Whiddy, Reverend Mahood, Bedell – translator of Holy

Scripture into seven languages, scholar-saint, bore imprison-
ment unto death when Christ blood streamed in firmaments of
1641, salute his sepulchre at Kilmore, serene under Cedars of
Lebanon he planted in his prime, turn away renewed, firmer to
attend fume of the branded drums, Catholic, Protestant, Presbyterian, Free Presbyterian, Methodist, Baptist, Anabaptist, Second
Baptist, Witnesses of the Lord, Seventh-Day Convertites, Adven-
tists and Jehovan Followers of the First Reformed, the roads
were thronged, hills a black commotion, gaitered zeal smote the
idle, the shameless, ponds, lakes, rivers, were drum, would
stampede deaf cows from deeps of the wood. Miracles had oc-
curred, and were chronicled, the year-awakened cows had, indeed, stumbled from the timber to create their own dewlapped
benediction (*Their progenitors, Sinner, stood by the Manger*), poor
hoofed dwellers of the field they gave witness, turned round
eyes – a wonder – at sunset to the Glowing Hill, bowed adora-
tion, that One Hill which, another land, another day, might have
been visible but here not to be seen – Stains of Sin had engendered fog, steeps of murk, recalcitrant night was everywhere – a
plague, spawning death, sickness, rheum and ague, spirit-ills,
every stubborn disregard for Wing Rippling the Water, night was
Infidel, Adversary, Beelzebub, Lord of Flies and Temple Harlot,
no matter, let be, let belief and distillation of The Word curtail infidel onslaught, miracles recurred, sheep were known to have
congregated where preachers renowned expounded text, feathered flocks came on Festival Days as the devout knelt, lark,
thrush, the wren, circled churches and sang while choirs gave
way, horses, in days before the motor-car, had, some Pastor
stranded, been known to manifest, perform the Samaritan deed,
melt into beneficence, and, these events commemorated, as they
dutifully were, Recent Testament to rival and augment The Old,
The New, cries of approbation rose, ovations swelling the, by
now, irremediable clamour tenanting the air, drag on weaker
vessels such, the boy thought, an ample deafness must be the
rapid and lasting consequence, but no, subtle accord, most of the

vulnerable wasted in the lungs, that roar ceaseless entered lungs of the timid, young and timid – especially at risk, and capitulant, one day walking the street, next week coffined, galloping consumption a fresh daily bread, and, fiercely nourished by mortality, judgment drum and lantern jaw trebled the stakes, missions multiplied, Special Auxiliary Missions on their raw tracks, chapels, churches, barns, were not at hand to accommodate flow untrammelled of admonition, followers, prodigals come clean, tents were ordered, in parishes remote and near tents flowered, here was cultivation of the Lord's boggy vineyard, there ornamentation of the crabbed slopes, for a summer's length pavilioned preachers out of the Saviour North harangued, to a cordal hush cataracts tumbled, multitudes marched in the sobered dusk to meet Light Vouchsafed, were swept by rapture of Born Again, moaned, wept, convulsed, lay down depleted and were carried in loving care through the night, *repentant* night: smirched Bosom of Astarte, hot Chamber of Ashtoreth, Temptress Night – jubilant thing now, creature awake and shriven, purged to the pith – Night, all present concurred, rejoiced and made consummate union with the chariot uproar, *Christ is here, bow and be healed*, the strong in heart, the valiant, processed towards The One, drawky lesser brethren buckled, gave, lungs, yea, lungs withered, wrinkled on the bough, a number took the blow on the exposed head, offered themselves – carolling – to the boreens, heather-bell, charred furze of autumn, the boy, the boy fell down, right ear blasted, mastoid mayhem, infection coursing straight for the brain, she gets there, prepare, child, to meet Lord Risen in naves of Beyond, earth crumbling and all its mansions.

Tusitala's dog

A farmhouse, rough, in the hills. He's on the first floor. The room has aspirations – carpet of quality, piano against that wall – but no mistaking he was in the arse of nowhere. Kingdom of the hill-folk, the whins. He stood at a window, looked down onto the bare farmyard, long disused. A stillness out there, uneasy. No people, no animals – bar an old dog, retriever, brown and curly, sitting against a wall to the left. In a doze, looked like. Something about that dog bothered him, hard to say exactly what. The dog looked all right, maybe a bit long in the tooth, in retirement almost, you'd say, and yet – wouldn't that condition, as a rule, rouse pity of some hue rather than perturbation? The perturbation grew, his notion that the dog carried threat, mortal threat, to put it bluntly. The yard was alive with flies – it was summer, yes. Buzz-buzz of the flies audible – even through the closed window, that window hadn't been opened with years. The dog moved. Dog shot out a paw, caught a fly in the open palm, and – like an ape – carried it to his mouth. Now: looking up suddenly at the spectator in the window, the dog winked. Nature of wink? Omnipotent. Intimate. Removed.

Tusitala's criminal past

He is living abroad, so as to keep out of the way of the father, a wealthy widower, overbearing, and a bully. He returns home to find his father has remarried, young wife by him, who's unhappy in the relationship. Because of this misalliance (the son indistinctly understands), he and father should meet. The meeting, matters being as they were, must take place on neutral ground. They face each other, accordingly, on a desolate shore. They quarrel. The son, stung by some intolerable insult, strikes the father dead, leaves the scene. The dead man is found and buried – the son is not under suspicion. He succeeds to the family estates, finds himself living under the same roof as the widow, for whom no provision has been made. At first, the two live very much alone, as people may after a bereavement. Gradually, they relax, and a friendship begins to develop – until (it takes no great time) it seemed to the son that she had conceived an idea of his guilt, she was watching him, testing him with odd questions. He drew back – for a while – but the attraction was there, he'd, again and again, drift into the old intimacy, and – again and again – be driven back by some suggestive question or some inexplicable meaning in her eye: she must know. The see-saw continues for a time – broken dialogue, challenging glances, unreleased feeling. One day he sees her – veiled – slipping from the house. He follows her to the station, in the train to the shore, out over the dunes to the scene of the crime, watches from hiding as she begins to grope in the eel-grass, and, presently, straightens with something in her hand – he couldn't quite remember what – but it was material evidence against him. At that moment, a fierce gust of wind intruded, whipping his investigator towards the brink of a tall dune. On the instant, he went to her rescue. They stood face to face, deadly evidence in her hand, his very presence in that place confirmatory proof. She made to speak but he couldn't bear that. He cut her short with trivial talk. Arm in arm, they return home – talking of he knew not what. They have dinner, he's voluble. Life goes on but 'When will she denounce me?' is now the consuming question. Today? Tomorrow? Next week? She made no move, their relationship found its old pattern except that she seemed kinder than before, while he, burden of suspense unrelieved, was slowly wasting. Once, losing control, he ransacked her room when she was abroad, and found, hidden among her jewels, the damning evidence. How strange, he thought, as he froze there, holding it, that she should seek, find, and keep, and still not use it. The door opened. There she stood. She, again, made to speak, again he cut her off. He laid his death-warrant back where he'd found it, saw her face light up at that, and left the room. The next thing he heard, she was explaining to her maid, by some dextrous lie, the disorder of the room. Something had altered. Now, at last, he was ready to speak out to her, he had no choice, the continuing tension would have his life. They've had breakfast together in one corner of a great sparsely furnished room of many

83

windows. She has resumed her way of teasing him with sly allu-
sions. He stands up. She stands, she listens to his streaming com-
plaints. Why did she torture him? Why did she not denounce him?
What was the meaning of her whole behaviour? 'You know all –
you know I'm no enemy to you – why this enduring torture?' He
fell silent. She looked at him, stretched out her hands to him – 'I
love you,' she said. 'Don't you understand? I love you.'

Tusitala's departure ...
Shortly before his death, he wrote to a friend – 'My skill deserts
me, such as it was or is ... I am a fictitious article, and have long
known it. I am read by journalists, by my fellow-novelists and by
boys.'

***Weir of Hermiston* (unfinished) ...**
They say of it that here for the first time he'd begun to write of
woman with some authority. The concluding lines read – 'He felt
her whole body shaken by the throes of distress, and had pity upon
her beyond speech. Pity, and at the same time a bewildered fear of
this explosive engine in his arms, whose works he did not understand, and yet had been tampering with. There arose from before
him the curtains of boyhood, and he saw for the first time the ambiguous face of woman as she is. In vain, he looked back over the
interview; he saw not where he had offended. It seemed unpro-
voked, a wilful convulsion of brute nature ...'

That evening – the wife gloomy wih premonition – he fetched
a bottle of their best Burgundy from the cellar, poured the wine,
toasted – '*A l'avenir!*' They made the salad together. Slick of oil and
vinegar, the green leaves danced. His hand snatched at his head.
'Do I look strange?' 'No ...' He was dead within hours.

You find them punitive?

I certainly believe they have to be watched. Trees met me one day, beautiful day it was too, the road downhill, lake-water – rife – to the left, no scarcity of trees but too tall, branches few, sky Persian blue beyond. Fine. Or awful. Or both. Neither! Let her spin. I spot – way up – on one of the trees a dot with an elbow, little bastard working away with his chainsaw, and 'Some stunt,' I reflect, sawing the branch that is his perch but shiver more for my own pelt, I could be, I am, in line of fire when that limb takes flight – the which is written – here she comes, huge, tree-size, knows me – that's part of my fret with trees, they know too much, she descends, guided muscle, speed of sound, slaps on the brakes height of a house, say, above me, noble fir, I recognize that *terre-verte* of the bark, hangs there, displays her – rare – endowments, 'How's that for weight, girth, juice, friend? Could ambition be of finer stuff?' I have nothing to say, unusual for me, *d'accord*. She resumes descent, and, for *coup de grâce*, this will remain till they prop the chin, for *au revoir* she touches down, bounces a couple of times, largo, the dying fall, Klemperer conducting, settles, serene, arranges herself in the long grass.

And the dwarf above – with chainsaw – Woodman-Woodman?

What about him?

How'd he make out?

No idea.

No interest?

Apparently not.

You have your incurious side?

'It has been becoming apparent ...'

The kerne?

Rough rug-headed.

So – I know you're not shy – did you make no approach at all?

To?

Terre-verte – in the long grass?

I was moved once to eat a tree. Taste. Better.

There's a jump!

Yes and No. I was in London – for whatever that's worth. The Other Place? Whether or which. There I am, stravaygin' near Shepherd's Bush, I notice a tree, soubrette birch. I've a fork in my pocket, sometimes I come prepared. On caprice, it seems appropriate to have a bite, taste that birch, Silver. So to it I go. The birch – as I've anticipated – is cooperative, more, welcoming, the birch wants this diner, a sliver of bark peels – itself, here's the wood, fork probes, finds it friable, on the way to muesli. I didn't gorge (not but I do). Collation. Light repast. That sufficed.

And?

Enjoyed it, I was glad – for the experience.

How'd it taste?

The birch? Tasted, not bad, tasted nourishing, tasted – wholesome.

But you didn't – in consequence – make trees a staple –

Of my diet – no.

Why not?

Don't know. Lassitude?

What was the response on that London street, crowded – I presume?

No one passed any remarks.

Amazing.

Not at all. I don't believe they even saw me.

How could they fail to see you?

Because – I suspect – of what I was doing. No one anticipated a man breakfasting on a tree – it was morning, did I tell you? – and therefore, could be some law of optics, no one sees the event.

Herod going forth –

Herod himself shall meet. Once in a while – Herodias. Salomé?

And never reprise of that *petit repas*?

No – but it started something – I shouldn't say 'started something' – it led to something – but what it led to was also a once-off.

My *faiblesse* the cul-de-sac?

What'd it lead to?

I was back in the Hinterland, October, seems to me now. I'm walking with a companion, possibly with her – that woman I've mentioned once or twice. Nothing much happening, just like life, only more so. Then I discover – right-hand side of the road, I see a carved head, rough-hewn, male, there it is looking at me, just across the ditch, a dunt – pleasant, more than pleasant, kick's protein-packed. 'Iron Age head,' I posit – I've studied that, the archaeological, these hills buzz Iron Age lavin's, the bogs in particular, heads mostly, they – for all their weight – chug to the surface. Stop! I realize – here's the *tour de force* – it's not stone, it's timber, carved from the living tree, that sycamore, spout from the trunk, your height or mine, the marks on the wood show it to be yesterday's work, today's, the maker could be watching as I inhale the piece. It has a primitive skelp, it's a fetish. ('All art is fetishistic' – Pablo P – 'but you can't be a witch-doctor twenty-four hours a day.' *C'est vrai*, Pablo.) I scan the prominent nose. Dog here somewhere. Sniffer. Seeing-Eye.

Did you touch it?

Wouldn't dare.

Didn't you want to get the feel of it?

The viewing satisfied – I'd had my ration for that day.

You returned next day?

No.

No?

Knew it wouldn't be there.

Why so?

That's their way. We'd meet again to a different note – if we were to meet at all.

And did you?

O, yes.

Click of the tape-recorder switched off.
Click on. Purr of tape – prolonged.
A voice – female: 'Italy is open vowels.'
Purr of tape – prolonged. Conversation resumes …
There was another tree once and if I were a painter I'd whistle, yes, and sing. It was night, and, yes, all cats are grey – but the contrary is also true, there's a night-vision other than High Command's Hi-Tech Installations, summon once more The Owl, night-world, moon-stroke that streams narrative, and that's the note for me. (Said to her the other evening – 'Always knew you were a story-teller.' You'd cross Gobi, comb Great Empty Quarter, to sip ensuing hazy smile.) Rising from bed of night, I go to greet the tutor tree, not, *Deo Gratias*, not a tall tree, rather a level-headed comfortably grown tree, conversable height. What was it about this tree – elm, by the way – that stopped the noise? Black specimen, unrepentant black, leafless, the bride stripped bare. 'Comfortably grown' – *vid. supra* – and pen an emendation: full-grown, trunk a dark pillar, the branches – black and blacker – stood out against the sky, tracery to stir the cripple, and, in summary, for all the black, all the pinions stripped bare, an immeasurable interior to the offering. The tree entered, left me – a stripling, old as the hills, the dips between. I rose then to the pure song of it, the heft, the wand. It lay in that royal black of candelabra, trunk. A bottle-green moved in the black, come-an'-go, rallentando. What altered (momentarily) your step? Word from a tree, night-song, the green in the black, how many trees in the wood, Tristan? Two. The green – give him the money, Barney! – and the withered.

You spoke of punitive back there – but –

But?

I've the tingle of – *rapprochement?*

That's your – sideline – angle. We're all suckers for the word *rapprochement*. I could caress it forever. But it's –

A lie? Usually.

A *bon-bon*. A *breá-breá*. I don't want to sound –

Acerbic?

Bilious. The conversation – somehow – continues. They won't stop.

The trees?

Won't let go. I would – I could – but don't. Inertia? Their profusion's The Ace between the wood and the bark. Know the shock – Neander-shock – of finding the tree occupied? Saw a hen-harrier – Athene written all over her – measuring me from a yew last Sunday, wondered a moment was I forgiven? Being watched from the tree – I understand now – is what I'm trying to cap. Saw the boy with cherry-sprig in gob fixing me from an ash, mountain ash, laden, lately. Month back found herself – the one I've mentioned once or twice – asleep in a sycamore, head settled on her left shoulder, the sycamore's keys jangled, and came my fit again. Plus there's a tramp – with silted eyes – squatting in a black alder down the road, shouts for alms. I do have some cheerful stories. I remember a spring, while back, I confess, too long ago, I saw the bridegroom, mounted, float – unimpeded, from heights of a Scots pine, red of the bark paging him, float umpteen storeys to ground floor, canter across the parkland, thence into a world.

The razors ...

A fox day. We'll go 'pullin' razors.' I will teach him how to find – and gather – the razor-clam. Suspicious assent. 'Why such hesitation?' 'Ingrained.' 'Don't you love the shore?' 'I revere the shore' – he capers – 'of The One-Strand River.' 'Where things happen, after all.' 'Thresholdy, you mean? Someone once told me all our stories are about Warrior getting stuck in the door of the *lios* ...' 'There goes an arm, there goes a leg!' 'For starters. They – we – must get into the *lios*, whiff of pussy, let me in, let me in, *lemmeinn*!' 'You've been?' 'Haven't you noticed my missing body parts?'

Hand-in-hand, we amble to the shore. Cattle keep an eye, asses horny bray the blues. His hands, he has soft hands of the dreamer, the pianist, the *peata*. 'You've the hands of a silk-merchant.' 'Music-teacher used to say I'd a lovely touch. "Awful pity", she'd add, "you won't learn." I suggested we try singing.' 'Anything come of that?' 'She didn't engage me. When you remember only the teacher's grief – a bad sign.' 'Was there punishment?' 'Odd wallop with a ruler. No – another minus – dominatrix in her.' 'Deprived childhood – do I smell?' 'By seven – Age of Treason – I'd decided Life was , most likely, a Serial Abuser.' '*Muishe*, aren't you great to be in it at all!' 'Put a spell on me – convert me – trance me – pixillate me.' 'I'm trying.' Fox day.

Spacious ballroom of the shore. Granada! Alhambra! Ebb-tide at the limit, spring-tide, wind assisting, meadows exposed. Shoes and socks off, trousers hiked to the knee. Plop of the wet underfoot, occasional squirt from a cantankerous cockle as we tramp past, razor-shells everywhere, ahead of us the razor-orchard. Mountains across the sound, their flanks moving clouds. 'What you spend your time at?' people ask him. 'Looking at the mountains, dreaming of the caves.' Climb the one, enter the other? But I know when to look through my fingers, be wise. Let the mountains, the caves, do their own talking, they will anyway. Salt air. View like this you could live on one meal a month. We could make love tonight.

We wade. About six inches of water, the ideal. The razors are under-sand, a few inches of water makes the sand more penetrable. And this art is about – in part – penetration. ('All art is penetration.' In part.) 'Move gently', I counsel, 'or you'll frecken the herd.' He obeys. I point to the water, flesh-coloured sand, reflective. 'See those concave marks?' He nods. They're everywhere. 'Breathing holes of the razor. He's perpendicular in the sand just under that mark. Slip' – I demonstrate – 'your hand into the water. Make a wedge of your fingers. Slide the wedge into the sand at a 45 degree angle – you'll hit the razor a couple of inches down there.' He's listening, watching, with the mouth open, can't believe in the under-sand orchard, few can. 'The razor'll freeze.' Fingers against the luscious shell of the razor, taste the fright in there. 'Now, bring your thumb into it – you have notably assertive thumbs – thumb over and down, get a grip on the razor.' I don't look up, monitor his assent, he was never at school till this. 'Now's the tricky bit. Pull – slow-air pull – and you'll feel, foot-suction, the clam pulling against you, tug-o'-war, he'll fight, but no rush, no hurry. Yank – you get the shell, lose the fish, ever have that experience?' Susurrus of his smile. 'Patience be the word.' Patiently, patient as an ant, I ease the razor's streaky pastels up through the sand, swirl in the water to free sand clinging, and up into the day. 'Here.' He puts hands on it, confirms it, stows it – delicate – in the bucket. 'See how it's done?' He nods – elemental salute to largesse beyond his ken. Wide open he is. Can be. When he takes the gallop. It takes him. 'The tide's on the turn, best time to get them.' 'Why?' 'They know it's the flood, their order returning, they relax the bit more.' 'Sweet Neptune.' He takes my hand, we sway there, lithe in the spell, everything's journey, Hyacinth.

'Try it.' My apt pupil. Gets the knack quickly, loses three or four, chews his vexation, learns to take the waking slow. The bucket begins to fill, pair of us active. Colour of those shells. Weak cocoa. Khaki. Pansy. Marigold. The garden. I watch him fall in love with the choreography. Breathing-hole spotted, chosen, stoop, the wedge, insertion, right, pulse of alert in the hidden below, thumb over and down and grip secure, and pause, still all the traffic from here to Fremantle, and lights change, and, supple bow above the stir of grains, coax, wheedle, collogue, plawmas brave doomed *croob*, and, let it take forever, back lifting – he has become arcs of our covenant, briny exhalation, now, razor into view, and wristy swirl, signature, cleansing of the water, and up and wonder – the treasure – and bucket receives. 'I'm learning – calligraphy.' We kiss above the haul.

I had him cook them. Steam is the mode, then garlic butter across the pearly philandering slivers. Licks the plate. Looses an interrogatory eye. 'How's it you never cook for me?' I said nothing, eyeing the line of cooks behind him. He sees me seeing them, gives himself to recollection – a tendency, if not (quite) an addiction. Bias will do. 'W – she'd lived among the Arabs – had a Chicken Pilaf to die for, X – with X, conservative by nature and therefore given to the *outré*, it was Lemon Soup – celebrated the width of Connacht. Y drove guests – as well as me – towards dissolution on the flavours of her Beef Bourgignon, Z – dare I term this an ascending curve? – she perfected through sorcery a Jugged Hare to nerve the timid, disarm the bold.' Pause for chambered echoes. 'But you never cook for me.' 'That a complaint?' 'Yes.' 'Don't you understand?' 'Tell me again – for the record, for the stone.' 'It's you I have to cook.' Great chefs of *la plus haute cuisine* fly past, honking like geese of autumn.

Grow young with me, *pièce de resistance* yet to be. After supper – fox night to follow the day – I take him again to the shore to watch the razors dance under – large of the moon. By the time we get there – place deserted, bars humming – the ball had found the beat. There they were, no care for shelter now, erect – or slightly tilted – on the playground lower shore, hundreds swayed to the silvery clarion. No wind. Sound – phosphoreal – of far waves. You didn't dare approach these glitterati, let them rear, pomp, twenty metres away. Different palette this time, sapphire, dahlia, Ingres' 1000 greys. A Dali – if he'd stayed with Bunuel. A Bunuel, Magritte watching, maybe. He'd – characteristically – gone uncharacteristically still. 'What you thinking?' Looked at me, back to the razors, our *corps de ballet*, moving and not, ghostly, substantial, clickety, wrapped in eternal silence. Far from enemies. Looked at me, eyes captive – for now. 'Your definition of *it* – as we were shelling the razors in the kitchen, remember?' So he remembers. Looks directly into me, and you'd wager, Here's a Child of Nature can't – but can't – go wrong. '*It*', you said, 'is a semi-colon.' Concord. Lovefest of the razors. We take the long way home.

Above, Below, the Plimsoll Line

Taking you underground, they don't give warning, steer you – as they imagine – kindly down gradually darkening stairways, saying not a word, aware – to the nth degree – that you will not enquire purpose of this descent because increasing fear prohibits such. Traffic diminishes, light weakens, dirt accumulates, sounds are ingrown. A young nurse – Probationer – holds your hand, she could be holding a soup-spoon, being elsewhere and not saying her prayers. Ruction *bonhomie* of *The Play-Room* is receding with merciless speed, spiced anarchy of Nurse Glynn, facial tufts and wirrastrua gob of the West, seeking to hold an urchin mob to rule. 'Arrah, *doant grab*' – large tin plate placed centrally on the table, 'I said it the last day, will yiz not *grab*.' Turns her resigned back. Genteel rattle of the plate. Grey head swivels. As usual. Plate bare. Secure in fists of the incorrigible, a dozen currant-buns tick like hand-grenades.

In the kingdom of shades thrives the hospital-barber, lagged pipes roof the tunnel to his door. He makes you welcome – 'Good man,' you can see he enjoys his work, feels for the proscribed, every skull, nape of neck, thrapple, different, differently infested, 'good man yourself, where'd you be from now, ye little *culchie*?' (The Probationer's missing.) Invoking confections of lather, hospital-barber balances the razor, cut-throat, from behind a contented moue delivers himself to that half of the boy's skull neighbouring the designated (right) ear, conducts it to distrained pinkish bone. Takes a mirror, gives the boy a better look

– 'How's that now to dazzle the ladies?' Boy blinks. Blanks. 'Give you a scrape anywhere else while we're at it? Curlies on your chest yet? Below *The Plimsoll Line*? Balls of your toes? You'll be grand – all before you like the wheel of a barrow.'

It takes five minutes. Less. The Probationer steps out of a wall, boy's led back to Ward 16. Below *The Plimsoll Line* – no, matter of fact, curlies – did you when you were me? – one or two sprouts, smudges of sprouts, smidgins of smudges of smidgins … Anyway. Learn something most days. Judicial click of the cut-throat, this stays, briefly; stays also perky legerdemain of the barber, anterior surgeon and blade of preparation, clearing the road. Stays most of all from that descent the serpentine pipes, fulsome lagging, Christ, smothery and knowing, they'd pursue the boy for years, fertile, lonesome, beseeching a hand, word, bit of the road, don't be afeard …

Next it's now. Stomach empty, bladder empty, bowels, all high expectations. Disappointed ceilings provide the view as a trolley rolls him to the table – that's what they call it, he has discovered, *The Table* – you're the meal. Another phrase he'll remember – *Under the knife*. Barbers, butchers, surgeons. Tailors something else – the scissors. Were they? 'You'll like this,' he's advised – there's a team, hooded, green-clad, about him but he won't, has no appetite for that tile-red pliable mask with its sugared vapours. Brief parley. He suffers it over mouth and nose, vanishes spirally from himself to roam a nether world – even as Togo Grahame, hard by, FRCSI, Master of the Royal Victoria (a fiver for Famine Relief) Eye-and-Ear Hospital, completes a routine tonsilectomy, flings the tonsils to his Labrador, Winston (who does for them in one gulp), pets an imaginary prize rose of his own canny cultivation, moves to the theatre adjoining. Mastoid child.

Fresh gloves. Thank you. Togo accepts the trepan, admires its circle of pikey teeth, positions himself to satisfaction, and bores through compliant bone just behind the burdened ear – the boy shudders, bad sign if he didn't. Togo to work. Standard procedures. Check pulse and breathing, heart-rate. Examination of the villain mastoid, something beautiful about the mastoid process – even in adversity – nipple-shapes own the world, drive the trains. Aetiology of this I see before me? Nipples will always cause trouble – roses much simpler, much better behaved – I grow, I blossom, I die, I resume – boy a bleeder, to bleed is human, to staunch the task of an expert assistant, how is the patient, cleansing, treatment, gauze ribbons to beat Banagher, pulse, heart, breathing, he lives, moves, two-hour job. ('What kind's this operation, Mr Grahame?' – the mother. 'No prisoners, ma'am, taken.') Well. Bit of a mess but you'll rise. In some cave of the buoyant dark, the boy's antennae register a dog complaining. That's Winston, exiled to the corridor. Tonsils, fine. Mastoid, slim pickings.

'Mastoid children', Togo remarked to Sister Mc Quaide over elevenses, 'are an odd bunch.' 'Children generally,' Sister Mc Quaide ventures – managing to loose a suggestion of children as bothersome interferers with delights of the sensual, she knew it entertained Togo to believe she kept her legs in a knot. 'Odd, yes,' Togo's smile collected the nuance, rictus of The Somme, the *summum bonum* of that smile but you're not the worst, Togo. 'You can tell at once they've selected the malady – tuned to their natures. That said, divide by two. There are those who flirt with departure, choose to depart – you can spot them on the instant, the other side has them. And there are those who flirt with departure for the value of the experience, return to ruminate. You can tell them also, quizzical something, they're an extra category of doubting Thomases, they *must* see, and they *must* believe, taking little byway, maybe something in it for *The Lancet*, what d'ye think?' 'Is Ireland', Sister Mc Quaide crosses her legs, those independent limbs free hosannas to Switzer's hosiery, 'getting to you at last, Togo?' The boy, Togo concludes, he has heard, enjoyed, indexed, her siren pirouette, this morning's child, spectacularly talkative under anaesthetic, you, Sister will be aware, is bravely pursuing his education.

Topics touched on by the boy (according to usually reliable witnesses) while on the table ... Trees; a desire in houses, one in particular, he could vouch for, to cut moorings, waltz a distance, settle by water; bumpy waste-ground behind a workhouse where, he had reason to believe, hundreds lay, ancestor skeletons, in shallow graves; fox-pelt hammered to a door in some priest's backyard; the names of three mountains – Loughanlea, *The Lake of the Cure*, with scholastic deliberation he translated each name for his daylight listeners, Taghart, *The House of Art*, and Dooish, *The Black Fort*. Also, he spoke of a clouded girl of whom a grandmother had apparently said, 'For a sieve in the ear, there's always a price.'

What was Sister Mc Quaide's price – *Does any man dream that a Gael can fear?* – Boss Theatre-Sister beyond compare, twin to The Archbishop, she was Queen of the May, June, July, winter valleys wide, expanded in the shadow of her brother's limitless authority but, let it be understood, not of necessity. Tall, of middle years, bold on her haunches, an eye to threaten and command. What won attention, silent, in truth, acclaim, was the tempered pallor of her face and the darkly beaming eyes, barn-owl in there somewhere, and, capping all, the head of doctored black hair, flaming black, combustible. The boy cannot from her remove his gaze. Would not if he could.

Deem her event, Eye-and-Ear the home of event, not primary event, that belongs to trees, lake, the Workhouse, to Eye-and-Ear the extension, deepening, orchestration of the ground-music, one evening in Ward 16, two ancients – hitherto quiet as chamberpots – spring to arms for possession of *The Second Decade of the Rosary*. Bliss of the sudden. Both – the humour is on them – commence the decade. Neither will pull back. While you'd fart, they're at it, *Hail Mary* mounting *Holy Mary*, evening prayer as assault, scourge, nine-tailed blasphemy, Ward 16 rises to it – *Up Tipp*, someone roars – *The Lord is with Thee* – more fool he, Carlow spectacled greybeard and raddled Wicklow sheep-farmer, locked, tear strips off other and *Blessed be the fruit of Thy coagul-*

ated kidneys, teeth bite to the bone *fruit Thy fruit Thy womb* fruit of Thy froth wombats for ding-dongs drowning Blackstairs Poulaphouca Seán O Dwyer and the burly Barrow, every bed in the ward now riding the sainted bore, *Holy Mary full – Rise it! – The Lord is with Thee, Blessed –* Blistered, pray for all bastards, bollocks, ancients will not, not for ticket to heaven, look at each other, fatwa blinkers on, *Ave, jihad*, devout, carbuncled, the confraternally vicious *now and at the hour of our* stitches popping *Hail Mary, wholly mine* and up yours too, bandages awry, fall back, flushed, evacuated, Jerusalem'd, will not acknowledge, never, the recumbent and speechless standing ovation.

Not a good month albeit not all downhill. Notes left under stones – always cherish you for that. (Soil is not stone on stone!) 'Concerning Bacchus: not the flash, child of grace, but the flow.' And again – without elaboration – 'Your striped tongue, your long eye.' That striped opens to the quick – it would take her to apply such a lance. The 'long eye', I had to vet more closely – not the brightest under my own microscope. 'Long eye.' The unspoilable word long. Applied to eye. Long-sighted? Cyclopean? Pineal third isn't a starter, clearly. What she's on to, I decide, provisionally, is my seeing, and keeping (above all the latter) world at a distance, while gambling sweepstake with colours, textures, declared runners, starters, non-starters, casualties at the first jump, and fillies in heat juicing at the gate. Weep for these, for yourselves and for your children, not neglecting intuitives grown inexplicably deaf across decades by dint of inattention.

Haircuts a no-no. She has permission to clip the teeth, incisors (you'll recall), which continue to yield the brown-blonde tufts. My dentist swings from despair to jubilation, despair that the 'growths' (his proprietorial term) resist, with ease, plethora of medicaments, jubilation that he has under surveillance – his sole responsibility – a condition heretofore unrecorded in the annals of medicine, ancient or modern. Why brown-blonde? The issue exercises him to palpitation. Because the focus of my unrestrained appetite for a period had brown-blonde hair, I tell him. And for the first time – his mooncalf innocence – he saw the blue in my beard. And blanched. Switched the conversation to (his proven crutch-topic) the issue of nutrition as it bears on dental health, varying diets across millennia, and – faultlessly – he makes his Bible Belt jump, ever forecastable, ever surprising – 'Our Lord, for example, I'd say had very good teeth now.' Long striped silence while we contemplate the pop-star grinders of Pale Galilean. 'I would not doubt it,' I cannot resist the veneered coda. Grateful nod. This dentist, my chosen, from an overflowing stable, took sixteen years to graduate. Picked him for that reason. Hysteria. Quite. Which, be certain, has its roots in the brown-blonde tufts. Which, of late, have spread to the tongue. (Striped.)

Now a dip. There are dusks and dusks in it. I can't say – nevertheless – that I've ever encountered the dusk benign. It's there, I accept that, I must, there are, have been, will be, gloamings that woo participation on the most positive terms, half-lights that are benediction, *la crépuscule* stir of an angel's wing. Once upon a time there was a dusk that played – I won't linger to scan that sentence. It's *scripsi*. For a long time now, dusk comes bearing ambiguous gifts: plexus, nexus, sexus loose distress flares. I wish it were other. I'm advised it's in my remit to change the matter. I acknowledge it's in my remit to change the matter. I loiter without intent. The monosyllable *dusk* weighs a ton.

It was *duskiss*, I heard a man say, and, for a moment, dialect tang reduced the load. Not for long. I'm abroad in the dusk, and confident menace tours the synapses. A lake convenient – one of these lakes will take me away – with hares playing on thin ice which covers it. Wafery I know from my congenital intimacy with cat-ice and related states of – flooring, call it. The hares are taking a chance, light-footed tho' they be, they encourage the reading – inspect those haunches – that they recognize their quandary, have, perhaps, been driven to it, some fatalistic tempo to their turn and counter-turn and stand tells all – there – leveret goes under, and, as to a horn, dusk thickening the while, hunters appear, men and dogs, barking of those dogs, resolute, focussed, gait of the hunters – even against the blur of evening – unforgiving.

I get out of there, make for home, upset for the hares, well, out of sorts. Questioning, anyway. Won't say severe – but concerned probing. Which – the plaintiff claims – is something. I have hare connections. I know the heron can kill the hare – I've witnessed the deed, went white to it, haven't forgotten that black hare, night of the stoat that bared her all, took my spoor. I've been requested to attend a bevy of pregnant hares in the Presbytery garden. (The Counter-Sign!) One of them asked, kindly – 'You know you're moving, don't you?' This was news to me (so much is). I've since agreed to the hypothesis but with a console of reservations, watched the hare – her warm back to me – face endowed altar of a midsummer ditch, and murmur *Introibo*: for a month after, I left the gun at home. This was registered. Eventually, one delays for me on the downs. I stretch to touch her brown of autumn. No. Wouldn't trust my hand.

Home. Recent events have followed me into the house, this is the law. Fine. It's a silence. It's a somewhere. It's an everywhere. It's pursuit, I can tell by my breathing. Switch on a few lights. Turn off the radio left yacketing to deter intruders. Mooncalf (more) innocence. Herod going forth. Herod returning. It's merely a question of where, which room for the explicit statement, the implicit (see above) is ubiquitous. The kitchen is clean. Bathroom – have a piss. Piss won't stir, in too much of a stew to piss. Reach for your catheter. Pray for a doctor, female, came to your door, middle of the night, catheter at the ready, claiming your phone-call just received. 'You look fine – but – drop your pants, love?' We who project, what we project, provide, by definition, the well-tempered hook(s). Reluctantly, already watered and foddered and long until morning, I sent her away. And have, o, backward look, since mourned such dereliction.

The living-room. Where else? You have arrived. And you know. Therefore hesitate to turn on the light. The light – of its own accord – obliges. Such a wilderness of politesse in that low-key click. Your living-room – spectacularly tainted. Cast your eye, don't be shy, your long eye, let it loose. Yes. There we are. Here we are. Mankeeper, newt, if you will, foot long, they come all sizes, stuck to the wall just above the drinks cabinet. Verrucose. Plumply still. Doesn't budge. Won't. New Brain, Mammal, Doughty Reptilian. We could be here a long day, Keeper. Gush of embers (under the curtain in lieu of door) from that verifiable room of unverifiable portent cakewalk unto this.

An innocent, the first-preference votes declared. Unholy innocent, a recount qualified. Sometimes he had the conviction that he was being got at. Again, please. That her essential function was to get at him. How could any relationship find purchase on that barbed fulcrum? Because of his attachment. To her. Probably. Her attachment to him. Certainly. Animal-vegetable-mineral. There are engagements that don't make the Saturday page of *The Irish Times*, never mind gilded centre-fold of *Social & Personal*. Rather, are. *A donnée*. There is something alluring about that. The given. We are a given. But the deep seduction – tell it plain – was the know in her eye. That, and her fury – which had magnificence. He wasn't wont to tremble. Before her wrath he'd core-tremble. Curious state. She had his number. That gave her moral authority. But she had that anyway.

'Get rid of those shoes, why don't you?' The voice, excellent thing all seasons, supportive in reproof. Well. He had a difficulty – everyone knew about it, the shoes had progressed to a cheerful notoriety. He'd bought them in Florence years back, and, agreed, they were beginning to show age. Patched fore and aft, heeled and soled so often – a walking palimpsest. Patina of 'past it' – ever renewable. High recommendation. Desuetude their strong point! He relished the paradox. 'They should go,' she returned to it. Everyone returned to it. What, tho', about his fondness for them? Loyalty. Tradition. The hoops of custom. Shoes – like people or cats or Lady Gregory's toothbrush – may command respect. Earn their entitlements. No. He would not be parted from the shoes – old boots they were, not shoes, or, you could say, fashionably (once) between shoes and boots, gusseted. Gusseted! (He'd bought them, the first day, for that adornment. And the cuntal slither of the word, 'gusseted'.) He'd keep them for a while yet, so informed her. She nodded absently. Absently – qualified by her mantic presence. Geomantic. He'd been forewarned but wasn't in attendance at the time.

The shoes vanished – *éist do bhéal, éist* – the famous shoes.

Dressing-room of the Swimming-Pool. The mode there was valuables into the locker (combination lock), shoes left to idle on the slatted bench, slats everywhere – some architect obsessed with dripping bodies. But shoes. Theft-rate in the matter of shoes was zero. Nevertheless, his shoes vanished. And, in their stead, appeared an expensive pair of new shoes. Was this somebody's venture of a joke? Act ('Wasp', as the grandmother had it) of God? His friend have something to do with it? In that case, she'd have needed male assistance, strict segregation along gender lines was the law, except in the pool, but that's another story. No, leave her out of it for the moment. Perhaps it was just a 'happy accident'. Don't rule that out. Altogether. Happy because his desert. For, for walking up and down, for keeping his balance, on uncertain surface of the meridian. The shoes, they were shoes, fitted wonderfully well. He'd go for them. Wore them home. He had new shoes. She'd be pleased.

Within the hour a knock at the door. A pair of detectives. Do come in. Just a few questions as they gorge – yes, gorge – on his footwear. Compliments on the footwear. Where, now, would he have bought those? He told them his story, nothing held back. This reply wasn't considered satisfactory. He learned – they were wonderfully open, as the police invariably are when they've all exits closed – that his own shoes had been left elsewhere in the dressing-room, Bench 168 (a notebook was consulted), and the shoes of Bench 168 – a noted Judge of the Circuit Criminal Court – removed. Could they, if he didn't have any great objection, inspect the shoes he was wearing. Certainly, officers. The shoes were officially identified as the missing property of M'Lud. The culprit scrambled apologies, explained all over again. They weren't listening. His shoes were removed from a bag, pitched on the floor. Grand. They bag the fine new shoes for return to the offended party. Depart. He was lucky it didn't go to law. The matter was hushed up. Which is to say there was a deal of talk.

It all left a heartburn aftertaste. He'd like to have asked her about it – but she was off somewhere. She'd a tendency to fade, evaporate, but, in any case, there was no need for consultation. He'd arrived at her position. Passed her out, you could say. He detested the shoes, the famous shoes were loathsome to him. He didn't have to brood. He acted. His apartment was by the river. ('Isn't everyone's?' she'd remarked when he'd sung that distinction.) He opened the front window, steadied himself. Right shoe: a buoyant *slán abhaile* upward curve to clear the street – *embonpoint* seagull jinks – discard plunges to the waiting flood. Left shoe followed. The relief. Wearing the plain honest-to-God shoes he'd just bought, he went for a walk. Had a drink in his local. The new shoes were noticed – he didn't mind the gibes. They'd soon enough forget about him and his shoes, fix on the next kerkuffle. M. and Madame Saylavee. A good pint.

He walks home. Pleasant evening. Turns on the TV, six o'clock news. His window is open – he'd left it open following his deed of valiant note. Windows are mystery – let's not go into it. About five past six, another brouhaha in the Balkans, the shoes – the famous shoes – flew through the window, as near simultaneously as makes no differ, shoes dripping mud, sewage, stinking weeds, unknown creepy-crawlies, clatter on to the glass-topped dining-table, skid the length of it, and invade an eighteenth-century china-cabinet – long in the family – smash the cabinet door, and uproot the shelf of Waterford Crystal secured therein: Waterford tumbles to the floor, *smidiríní* scatter, baying the Revolution.

For the longest time, he sat there. He could tell – it seemed to him that he could tell – smell – proclivity in motion. His. Perhaps, if he didn't move, it could be postponed, directed elsewhere, persuaded from volition. He may have passed out. The dusk caught him up, the necessitous dusk. He rose, left the apartment, made enquiries locally. A fishing-tug on the river. Expensive gear. The shoes engage the gear – or the reverse. From the skirmish, inordinate damage. To commence. Thereafter, rage. River-rage. The Captain hurled the shit-faced shoes – boots – chancres – from the deck. They made for an open window. His. He would – he must – he did – compensate the fishermen. Would they compensate him for the

Waterford? He didn't pursue it. The shoes were becoming an affliction, were crucifixion. How strange life's sudden promotions, demotions.

He was at once astonished and blasé. That blasé was an achievement. Maybe a lie. A needful lie. Concentrate, son. Bury them, he decided. It seemed – comprehensive. A spade, earth, inhumation. Let them rot. Fortunately, a quadrangle of tiny gardens went with the apartment block. Not a gardener, he still had his plot. He bought a spade, and, one evening as the light fell, went down to the garden. Shame the devil, it was later, it was night. As well do it by night, snoopers abound. A waxing moon, in which he rejoiced, it was a plus to be able to see what he was at – and the flashlamp would have been egregious. Moon, however – when would he learn – dispenses her lantern favours to the lilt of universal suffrage. An officious neighbour spotted him, and thought it a good to call the police. He was about to inter the shoes when they arrived. Care to come along to the Station. Interrogation – the spade, his new spade, shining in the fungal light of the holding-cell. He kept repeating – 'I was only going to bury my shoes.' They wondered about that. It seemed an odd occupation. Would he like to stay over? This was gratuitous – but they must put the knife in, he was now on their list, he had a record. Release the next day. The Press had been alerted. Photographers present. 'The man who wished to bury his boots.' He was on the road to the pillory. He was there.

By now he could have murdered them. Can you murder your old boots? Yes, with ingenuity. He calculated, decided. Taking the malevolent boots, he drove out of the city and into the mountains. A clear head is a great asset in the *bearna bhaol*. Checking now and then to see that he hadn't been followed, he discovered a remote valley, not a soul, not a sheep, not a titter of birdsong. The place was eerie, he should have moved on, but he was in a hurry. He found the desired pool – it had that consoling look of the bottomless. Flung the boots into it, they sank without protestation. He drove home. A man free of his encumbrance. Plural.

104

World, if, once in a while, it would agree to simplicity. The city water-supply came from a reservoir two miles away. By mischance – or baleful intent – or some hard-rock jester star – the shoes negotiated a mazy route to the water-system, even negotiated a complex web of pipes that led directly to the innermost workings of the filtering process – there they were happy to settle – and gum the works. Alarm signals. Workmen. Engineers. Divers. Boots. The famous boots. Knock on the door. Come in, gentlemen. Fourth Estate boisterous in the corridor. Front-page (a first, oddly enough) picture of the shoes. The Courts. Substantial fine. 'Didn't you see the notice forbidding the disposal of litter – with specific reference to the fragility of the Filtering Installations?' 'No, I didn't.'

It was time to burn them. Incinerate. Scatter the ashes. But they were still sodden. All right, dry them. He put them on the balcony to dry in the sun. Now, a dog. There's always a dog. Next door. The dog took to one of the shoes, the left. Thieved the object of affection, carried it to the adjoining balcony, had a great time there playing with it. Until – it's written – the shoe falls from the balcony, strikes a passing child, and the child's knocked unconscious. The shoe's recognized at once. A crowd. Police. Uproar. He went down to do – whatever he might – or could. As he arrived, the child stood up. It was the child, eyes of borage blue, he'd met before – cherry-sprig in mouth. 'Long time no see,' said this resilient chiseller. And pointed. To the dog above on the balcony. All eyes followed. The dog winked. The crowd got outa there. He was alone. Culprit Esq. No, he wasn't, ever. Other side of the street – Herself. Her Indoors. Focus on her slender neck. Scar there – he'd never seen before. Star-shaped. That passed into him like a Sibyllary spear.

Nothin'd Do You

The mother woke in her sleep, Himself snoring his trapped snore, bedroom crowded. Before she'd do anything else, she'd get rid of the snore. Raising herself in the bed, she took hold of his upper lip, held it firmly between thumb and forefinger, and, twisting clockwise, counted three – the snoring stopped, old country cure, variation on a trick used to quiet uppity horses. She looked about her, the mill of them – 'Who gave leave for this?' she asked mildly but nobody passed the slightest. Saunders was there and Mr Grahame of the Eye-and-Ear and Dr Ryan, who delivered the girl, and Jemmy Cullen, cap back-to-front, sitting in a corner, bicycle beside him, what was left of a Black Nelly. You could tell wind through trees. 'Dr Ryan will give us a word or two,' said Saunders. Ryan was by the fireplace, looking at the empty grate as if he'd never seen a firebrick before. Right shoulder stooped, excitable eyebrows, and rubbing the stunted hands, he parted the air, commenced – 'I was *not* in my cups. The wean, bantam-weight, slipped through these fingers and on to worn carpet. When I pick her up, she's right as a trivet.' Rubbing the hands, parting them, he stepped back. Stinking of whiskey.

'We'll now have an interval,' Saunders again, 'or – put it another way – a short interlude.' The mother got out of bed, hitched her nightdress close, went to her knees, and prayed they'd leave or, at the very least, have the manners to explain this presumption. But no. Saunders – 'To your feet, ma'am, this is *your* prognosis' – ushered them all to the front window, Jemmy Cullen dragging the Black Nelly. Saunders drew the curtains, opened the cranky shutters, let up the blind. Moonlight washed the lawn. A big lump of a crow dropped from the sky, hit the grass, lay there, dead meat. On the trot, an old woman came on-stage – that was the feel of it – gathered the crow, God alone knew how, with her left ankle, exited under the trees. 'I've a wee woman to see.' Jemmy Cullen planted himself on the bicycle, rode out of the room in a hurry, 'Gristle questions – and the fe-male women have eggs that know!' They heard him cycling down the stairs, bumpy passage, but he stayed in the saddle, divil's own, divil's luck.

Saunders, smoothly in charge of the proceedings, signalled to her. She pulled down the blind, closed the shutters, drew the cur-tains across again, debating her compliance but unwilling, or un-able, to contest it. The word *agony*, word she'd never entered, coasted her lips. Was this the meaning? She put a hand to her mouth, the fingers came away bloody, why blood now, she'd – unbeknownst – bitten her lip, a habit, not a habit either, but not unprecedented. She sucked the fingers clean. Taste of blood, lukewarm, slippery, no taste, no smell, that maybe for the better, thank you, *tabula rasa*. She checked her mouth with the left hand, lips dry, no sign of blood. You imagined the whole thing, you'd like to bite blood, your lips, measure that lukewarm-slippery, might tell you something you've forgotten or never knew. Smell of blood. She'd give a thousand pounds to learn the smell of blood. Ten thousand to let that chalice pass.

'Ma'am?' Togo Grahame stood before her, cream rose in the left buttonhole, war-medals on the opposite lapel, he polished them with his well-pressed sleeve. 'You're troubled', he probed, 'by that crow from the welkin, hostile fire, and the hag as *Ambu-lance Corps*, weren't we all?' 'Wasn't even thinking of it,' she lied, half-lied. 'It was the left-ankle *prestissimo* upset me,' he swept on, 'bit too *Celtique* for my liking.' A hand on her shoulder, spoke in-timately – 'I've been talking to the maid – tracked her to Kilburn, found her in a dingy return-room darning her cobwebs. I put it up to her. She denied everything, then broke down and acknowledged she'd gone inside to pen a letter to a friend, long letter dashed with felt tears. She is – need I add? – uneasy, distracted, and deep regrets. Any comment?' She turned away.

And there was the maid, Maggie, standing between her and the side window. Arms folded, she was forever one for folded arms. And the dirty apron. Wisp of a thing with dull carrot-red hair, something close to a cast in the watery left eye. It was the expression on the slut's face she'd have liked to fathom. Foolish now. Foolish always. *I don't know what I'm supposed to do next –* that puss on her. People don't change – especially if they're slow, Maggie, do they? Day she's alone in the house, there's a knock on the open front door, Aunt Delia in from the country. 'I'm in the bath,' screech from upstairs. 'Have you no towel handy?' 'All right.' And the eejit appears at the front door bare naked with a towel on her head. Why'd they employ her the first day? Have to be badly stuck, and they were. 'Show us that right hand, Maggie.' Maggie extended the hand, and the mother checked. Patch of sweat on the palm, same old Maggie. 'Wasn't my fault at all – the child,' she mumbles now through the jennet teeth. 'It's all right, Maggie.' From some cellar, the courage came to let it be said.

Dr Ryan, now openly sucking his whiskey-bottle, had something to show them – 'I have not imagined it,' he led them across the landing to the bedroom opposite. 'Other times I believe I could not *but* have imagined it. It beggars prescription. Would you mind?' He pointed to the western window and she obliged: curtains, shutters, blind. Bright moonlight gaped. *'Voilà!'* Ryan waved grandly. The lake – from its familiar position a hundred-and-fifty yards away – came towards them, stopped just the other side of the garden. Occupying, by that point, about one-fifth of the grounds, it flashed assertion. Set on a stone, well out in the water, they could see a figure, crude figure, like out of Africa. Three stones, one on top of the other, shapeless – but a man, reasonable assumption, looked like. Or a woman. 'Re-markable offering' – it drew, barbed, from Saunders. 'Untitled,' Ryan managed. And they were back in her own room.

Himself where they left him, dead out, snore discovering its camber again. Vindictively, an artery in her neck tugged at self-possession. She steadied, would say something, did, out it came, surprised her. 'One day on a beach I flung a stone for the dog to fetch – and he did, came back, stone a fish in his mouth.' This earned a doubtful spatter of applause. Ryan sat on the commode and began to weep – 'I am haunted by that triptych,' he told them. 'Not sufficiently, perhaps,' Togo Grahame reprimanded, and asked the doctor to leave – which he did, saying as he went on to the landing, 'I am a presence in this house – and proud of it.' He stumbled – the racket indicated – several times on the stairs, father a toper before him, wife a cow.

The snoring dimmed. Is this life mine? 'The only girl,' Saun-ders sat on the edge of the bed and glanced, idly Consultant air, at Himself sleeping. 'Is it possible you'd had your fill of it – gen-erally speaking? Such planes of rectitude', he took in the father again, 'in that Roman nose. You selected an Elder, nothing would do you, going forth we meet ourselves. What I'm getting at is this: was, push come to shove, *swerve* your binary measure? You pray more than most, from short skirts true believer, were you, I must ask, in the body?' 'I don't know.' 'The mountain shelf has its gelid attractions,' he purred. She remembered she'd forgotten something, crossed the landing to the other room, saw again the stone figure growing from the water, pulled the blind, closed the shutters, drew the curtains. Caught breath.

And, impelled to delay, listened. Saunders talking to Togo Grahame in the room beyond, parenting of Saunders's voice, she began to like him more, challenge of his posh tone. 'There are cer-tain things', he was saying, 'she recalls but won't readily address. A pool once, about this time of night, brimful of waiting swans. Then a note: *No theatre, ever, unless someone present.* And, another time, in the cabbage-patch, fifty, or more, butterflies lifting into the air, inflating, swelling to newpaper proportions, then falling, quite understandably, unable to sustain flight, all collapsed back into cabbages. You'd wonder.'

She tiptoed across the landing, girlish for a moment or tip of such longing, looked in at them. Both nodded – expectantly. Himself still out of it, Roman nose and all, her nominated Elder. 'You forget some bits', she said, 'and suckle more. An owl glanced at me once, mediatrix thing, gold, brown-red, eyes – buffed, you know the way it is with owls. And, later, one summer, a haystack. The father, a bee-keeper, was standing beside me, honeypot in his hands. It would be about one o'clock in the day. And I saw – told him – the haystack begin to smoke, go on fire, turn – seconds – black bed of flame. All he'd say was, *Happens*, gearcaile, *happens in the heats of summer*.

By Berry's Lake

He took her for a walk by Berry's Lake where the slaughter was in '98 – thereafter wiped from the slate, rebel turncoat with good connections jooked his way out of jeopardy, powdered his periwig, swore oaths to the Crown, and, that managed, found it useful to cancel official record of the particular engagement where he'd fought for Liberty, quickly done, all reports of it in files of Dublin Castle stolen or destroyed, and didn't it pay, grandson, no less, of the same rebel reformed, becomes Lord Chief Justice of Ireland, Baron Somebody – you couldn't make it up – ever dander back, M'Lud, to enjoy the scenery, red swatches in the water forever from blood poured down the slope that day, pikes in the ground, skulls, hacked bones, patches where animals – never mind the hunger – refused to graze, drew back, knew the differ. 'What was the fightin' about?' She scanned the lake. 'The English.' 'What's the *English*?' 'They're from England.' 'Kem on holidays?' 'Wore out their welcome.' 'Bad cess to them!' (Phrase picked up from the mother a week back, now being practised on an hourly basis.)

It was a middling day. Earlier mizzling, not drizzling, *mizzling*. Before that drawky. Stridable day might yet come to be. They flung themselves on the grass and searched for whatever might turn up, swords, maybe, medals, boots, hatchets, daggers, and the like. Bullets. But found little. The boy, patient, kept the head down, pooched for signs, found diversion in the different grasses, blue-eyed, scutch-grass, water-grass (drops of), clovers

white and red, double-daisies'd take on to give Confirmation –
and thus didn't notice what the girl was at. When he looked up,
she was flying above the lake, swimming, it resembled, arms extended and graciously paddling. Her plaid skirt swayed in the
breeze, mares' tails in the sky beyond. He called to her.

'What's in the lake?'

'The well.'

'What's in the well?'

'A bottle.'

'What's in the bottle?'

'The cure.'

'For what?'

'The craw-cree.'

'What's that?'

'A pain.'

'Where?'

'The heart.'

That's your sister up there, Sister Sustenance on her flying
trapeze – a buoyancy descended that could have whipped him
aloft to join her but, timid, he held to his moorings, that hour
would come, he'd know it and he'd meet it and, if he didn't, then
he'd miss it and be left standin', never learn to shiver, turn to a
stick and break in two under the wheels of an ass-and-cart on a
wet night, he wobbled.

'Anything else in the lake?'

'It's alive with the dead.'

From her fine element, she floated down, stretched herself beside him. He made her a grass ring, a rush bracelet, a bog-stick
necklace, arranged these on her. She belonged. '*Merci beaucoup*' –
caressing the figayries – and back with her to the craw-cree.
'Man walking the road, whinging, I said – *What's up with you?*
Says he, paw to his heart, *I've the craw-cree, child*. Wouldn't take a
sweet.' She played the grass ring, its own emerald. 'I love you,'
jumped out of the boy. 'Shure I know.' 'Will you marry me?'
'Might.' 'Someday?' 'Might now.'

There were three ponies in the field, a black, a white, and a piebald. They'd remarked the girl as she flew above the lake, made nothing of it, went on grazing. Now, however, they came, as one, to introduce themselves, nostrils winking, and a sniffing-match began, nosings and head-neck confabs, shy for starters but it shifted. 'I'm in line for a foal, green, with five legs,' the girl informed each of them, the ponies nodded, one hinnied, and the gambol opened from there, became a dance, shape to it, figures of eight the dominant, the horses created it, boy and girl found the beat, let their hands contribute, lightest touching, *right-left – right-left-right* – undulations of the black, white, piebald words of a song, on it went, gavotte, springiest dressage, trip of hands, five of them slaking a thirst until, contented, the ponies upped and out of there, left ceremony, and field, world, could be, curving back into themselves, ponies made of light, light made of ponies, the three slipping through a blackthorn hedge like it was blossoming silk.

No bother passing the time, look about you, tell stories of what's to be seen, and, beyond that, the what's not. 'Who made them hills?' 'The valleys between.' Whisk of a worn riddle. They counted the hills in sight, eleven and a half, explored names for the different lie of them – the boat upside down, the cone, the tabletop, corkscrew, twins, the breast, that the most beautiful. Tabletop had the track of a fort, said to be an O Reilly fort, sometime lords and ladies gay, minted their own money for all the good it did them, last of the clan – Planter Lantern-Jaw now the boss – took to the moors and shoughs, sloes in a purse, polishing them, checking them every so often to see if they were more or less, young lassie astray, said good-bye to herself one night, bog-hole handy, and she tired of the road.

'It's a bone,' the boy surfaced from sway of the hills and O Reilly misfortune. 'What's a bone?' 'Craw-cree comes from a bone pushing at the heart.' 'Kill a body?' 'Could. Wait a minute.' He went up to a cottage at the head of the field, around the gable and to the back door. Knocked. Asked the woman who answered would there be any chance of a jamjar, bit of a paper, a few matches. She measured him up and down, touch of nature in her, he was lucky. 'Making a cure, are you?' 'Give it a whack.' 'The craw-cree?' 'That crab, aye.' '*You're* not carrying it?' Shook his head, simplest thing, he knew he was a natural carrier for every germ that was. She gave him the bits and pieces. 'Mind yourself.' Would he like a sup of fresh buttermilk? Not now, thanks.

He returned to the girl. By then, he knew, was beginning to know, what he was at – but nothing said. He took off the girl's blouse, lowered her vest, she watched him light paper, place it in the jar, set the open end to her chest, count of ten – paper burning, purls of smoke trapped in there, pull the jar free. There was a loud report, enough to frighten a blackbird close by. Peaked, the boy emptied black flakes from the jar, saw them depart on wisps of breeze. Vest settled, blouse back on, she looked at him – 'Better now, are ye?' Knew she'd been his stand-in. 'The bit,' he said. That was the hour he acknowledged, no let, she was his lightning-conductor, mutual acknowledgment, and binding. She took the jamjar, found a single black flake in the bottom of it, somehow diced it on to her fingertip, sailing her own secrets blew it away.

Stretched themselves again. Lake for spectacle. You could see red in the water there, bright as the day it splashed. A spy's – always on offer – spy's handsome work did them in. There he is, pipsqueak ache about the lugs, he'll be home before night, live till God fires a stone at him. 'Has Jemmy Cullen the craw-cree?' she wanted to know. 'Riddled.' 'Joe Armstrong?' 'Hard to tell with Joe.' 'Taylor the barber?' 'Where's *he* traipsing to?' Fifty yards away, more, an English angler to be seen – sergeant-major wattles the giveaway – moustached holy fret of him emerging from a clump of reeds to the left, putting down the boot, and up the field, a thing demented – monster pike go for him? – found a gate to bark his knees on, falls the other side, and see you later, no looking back.

Baked silence. The pair of them – insurance – joined hands.

'Here it is.' Noise coming at them, shouts and shots and screams now. Out of nowhere, it rose to a cracked meelya-murder, a flail, death-moans in it, howl in the whip of blood, screech of no escape. It was next them. They flung themselves flat, held each other, held tighter, not breathing, let it build to a plateau, butchery come back, licence granted in gaps of time, took its chance this day, spun black red and whirled paunched blues, drenched a broad swathe, then, quickly as it reared, roared on, to a beldam whine cleared the brow of Rebel Hill.

Doh! Doh-So-Mi-Doh ...

Salubrities of singing celebrate. Such a voice, beautiful voice. You must sing. Are you a crow? Whose turn? *Shsssshhh* ... Quiet. *Moya, My Girl ...? Red Red Rose* ... The bould Rabbie ... Ceaseless the singing. Tenors (monarchs of the glen), baritones, sopranos (flighty), contraltos, Tom Moore and Percy French, Balfe and Stephen Foster, the skills were so-so, whimsical, at mercy of temper – good or ill, sore throat, hiccups, hernia, thrush, pride and false modesty, yet the singing persisted, one with living, natural as handshakes. And, for all its familiarity, earned an ear, there was more to it than at first appeared. The real presence of the singing was that in the offering the story of the one became visible, stepped from veils of woebegone, paused, slipped away again out of all knowing.

'Mc Breen's Heifer'. The father loosed it in his predestined tenor – sang oratorically, chest out, hands in the pockets, and pinned his gaze to the mirror above the sideboard, not to admire himself but for something to watch – while he concentrated on the diction, let it be just so, Papal Count John Mc Cormack his mentor and his muse – *O, Mc Breen had two daughters and each one in tu-uuuuurnn / Was offered in marriage to Jamesy O By-rrrrrnnne* ... Proper enunciation clipped the heels of Mc Breen's heifers, drover dyspeptic on the *qui vive* for any least transgression, assistant drovers up ahead to make assurance double sure, compel plaudits of Count John, *Clarity of the diction, O*, words of the poet, *Clarity, clarity of the diction, O* ...

Middle of the third verse, the boy sat up. He was in a disused corner of the local hillside graveyard, yews just so, plots likewise and gravelled paths, wrought-iron gate to the premises freshly painted, a smirky laurel-green. His eyes hopped. From a festive canopied platform on the brow of the hill, the father and Count Mc Cormack, cummerbund tastefully hung, were performing for a large audience of excited tombstones, resident and visiting, they'd come from all over, ditches thronged with dawdlers jostling for the best value. Yewy yews. Aware of intruder status, the boy took refuge in a yew, watched, listened. *Ave, Maria* commencing – *Aw-vay, Mar-e-e-e-e-e-e-e-awwwh, graw-aw-aw-aw – awt-s-e-e-e-awh play-ay-ay-ay-ay-nawwwh* … The pair sang in perfect harmony, and the diction – racked vowels, chopped consonants, had an Inquisition certitude and flair – *Domm-e-e-e-noose tay-ayyyy-coooom … Tay-coooom … TAY-Coooooooooooommm* … 'Are you all right, sonny?' He'd been spotted, friendly enough tombstone, tall, Connemara marble. 'And you thatched like an onion!' The boy checked, he was wearing five overcoats, the conversation was cut short by a battery of applause – patrons hurling themselves against each other in a fury of acclamation, father and Papal Count John, hand-in-hand, bowing to the cannonade, smiling faintly, and faintly smiling, on all the graven devotees.

'Shanahan's '. The mother would on no account sing, would recite, another kind of singing, stood by the red mahogany table, and, even before recitation began, was on the way to becoming the image of herself – see, on the mantelpiece, studio picture, three sisters, playing-cards in their hands, a camera on the table – first of those three, young woman hitched to the far-off – *This is the tale that Cassidy told – in his hall of sheen with purple and gold / Told as he sat in his easy chair, chewing cigars at a dollar a pair* … her characteristically regulated drawl searching for – and finding – fond caresses in the phrasing, relishing displacement, exile her name and sutured nation. Wait. She's only warming to it, something in her that will take on to change climate, juggle calendars. Second verse – early as that – *The cathedral round the corner and the*

Lord Archbishop to tay / Shure I ought to be stiff with grandeur but me tastes are mighty mean / I'd rather a mornin's mornn' in Shanahan's Ould Shebeen – second verse mists the bookcase, light drizzle begins to fall in the room, and – presto – mother multiplied by three, demure flapper of the picture, mother here present, and the woman with grey hairs or none, years, not that many, ahead, standing exactly where now she stands under a cerise umbrella, pillbox hat, a shimmer, thinking of nothing, nothing thinking of her.

'*A Neansaí mhíle ghrádh,*' Father Maguire, mearing dissolved, sang too – '*a bhruinneall 'tá gan smál*' – golfer's bluff regard, longest drive in the diocese, settled on a many-coloured vase beside the mother, her pettish hand, indeed, upon it, His Reverence's focus never relinquished that vase. And, to spool of the love-song, he unwinds. Preacher thrust and pulpit woe leave him, he sloughs clerestory noblesse, a splayed fox in his decorous parlour abandons mauled durance, turns to the rogue roamer with hoops-black-and-green, Reynardine plus fiddle-and-bow, master-singer, finding the notes for an adopted son who, responding to the call, waltzes the mother in lover vein, escorts her to the Gardens of the West, a dimple shows, hers, the maple floor – tongued and grooved for secret nailing – supples foot-soles, calves, knees, delinquent thighs, and *slán beo* 'Shanahan's Ould Shebeen'.

Bannion. Asked to sing, as she frequently was, the girl would utter the one word – *Bannion* – and leave her suppliants satisfied, room sated. This was the girl at her reverberant best, girl as rosined bow, she could contrive to make of those two syllables a song that *flahoolachly* embodied her. She had assistance. From brave full lips and coy, she invoked 'Three Lovely Lassies from Bannion' – Delia Murphy's celebrated single, ogler oglin' her wiles, peddlin' sheep's eyes – decorating the space with three and thirty beauties from Bannion and townlands adjacent, orchestra in support, Delia – *chanteuse fabuleuse* – and wife, it was said, to our Ambassador to the Holy See, Delia, *a stór* – stroking the air with *leannán* wand, leagued with the girl, The Powers, the troubled, the blessed, all those who dared – even for one solitary misshapen moment – to take the floor.

Asked to recite, the boy would say he was thinking. 'About what?' 'My next illness.' This reply never palled. No gloss requested. Don't overwrite. That was his current manifestation. In a previous state – he writhed to confess – his party piece had been a *Prayer for the Canonization of Blessed Oliver Plunkett ... O, God, who through the labours of Blessed Oliver Plunkett, thy martyr and bishop, didst preserve the Irish people in the Catholic Faith, grant through his intercession abundant favours and graces that he may soon be glorified by thy Church with the honour of Canonization, through Christ, Our Lord, Amen.* Applause, applause. (You pay – and he knew it – for such collaboration.) 'Has it pat!' (Never mind, they, too, would rue it.)

Stop Press. They were all waiting – boy and girl waiting with the rest – for Miss Vera Mc Getterick to take the biscuit. Miss Vera now to her feet. Now singing 'Danny Boy' in a tethered un tholeable soprano, and weeping as she sang, defiant, never the handkerchief refuge, never, let them fall, stream. Adults composed, looked down, but the boy and girl pursued, insatiable, every tear, tracked them, tasted, tested for salt and clay, the pipes, the pipes calling and soughing at beck of the *uilinn* for Vera, titled Aunty Vera, Assistant Matron in the Big House twenty miles away, *hurlamaboc* of those bellwether corridors snapping at her skirts, distracting her, but greater than any other distraction – now and forever – her own high predilection for fatality.

La femme fatale. Here incarnate? Men, it was known, dropped in her vicinity – and, in a manner of speaking, nothing intentional. A fine strapping man engaged to her (single *Intended* in a lean procession of decades) took sick leave a week before the planned nuptials – and courtesy of his own legally held handgun – did away with himself. Another lovely man, friend of long standing, fell dead because Vera's parked car – she'd stopped to chat – engineered, as it must, an accident, tractor and lorry punctual from nowhere to assist calamity. And there were others, suspects, confirmed cases. They were not forgotten. Silken black pennants fidgeted on their behalf from Vera's hyperactive wrists as – riveting hand-maiden of the shades – she led her Danny Boy the fraught winding ascent to his mullioned and sidelit cenotaph – *But come you back when summer's in the meadow* – homage incommensurate, proportionate, irreducible – *But come you BACK* – no peak of lamentation she would not, bosom churning, scale – *But COME YOU BACK* – scale, confront, from its cold ledges refuse refusal, while nothing nothing nothing stirs, not a leaf, all the valleys hushed and white, condolence *per omnia saecula* and Yes, she shivers, Yes, and Yes, yes, yes …

I was westward bound to search for her. She was in the car with me – liquid, solid, neither. She was the panties left in the bed – hypnagogic intoxicant – to engage pleats of linen, turn up weeks later between mattress and bolster, duvet and bouvez. Whipster in me had brought them along. Plastic bag. The ribboned proof! Just to see her face. Would she have changed. Yes. It wasn't that she never stepped twice into the same river, she was the river. I wanted her to be – one with me. I wanted her – mercies. Chastisements. Mild, please. 'Your bone gaze,' she wrote a month ago. Or two. Three. More. 'I will not be your veiled octoroon.' And the intonation – or was this my ear with no sieve – intonation stirring all the veils that ever nuzzled albescent octoroon.

Of the journey I remember Maynooth with its insomniacal spires, Galway's buttermilk salutations, no more. I arrive in the town where I have reason to believe she is. Where I know she is. I park the car, walk the main street. Torpor of the off-season tourist-trap – but for me carnival hour. There's a December volatility that should never be resisted, it must have to do with the solstice, viral visitation – it possesses me. I should perambulate the town, old haunt, make that opening statement. I do. A dance. People look at me, their eyes say – 'There's a stranger – whom we should know.' *Correct!*

I know where I may make initial enquiry. She has an uncle – o, fortunate uncle – who keeps a tavern. I find the premises. Enter. Behold the uncle, back of the bar. Oriental poise, enigma variations. We are expected. Being the unexpected, always expected.

'Yourself, is it?'

'Nobody else.'

This man is my Zen Master, holds my life. So be it. Casual chat. Winter storms. Musicians dead. New airport. Reticent fire listens. In that fire salute, burning, the topless towers of Ilium.

'Any sign of herself?'

'In here yesterday.'

'In good shape?'

'The best.'

'Where'd I find her?'

'House rented out there in Errislannan. Know Errislannan?'

'Sortov.'

Directions are simple. They always are. In a way. A right. A left. Hundred yards along. No boreen. It's by the road. Can't miss it.

'Check first with Molly Daly's,' he adds. 'The restaurant – she does be in and out there.'

I'm on the street. Daly's Restaurant is quickly told. The place is shut for the off-season but Molly Proprietaire, from the doorstep, is monitoring my approach. She's not surprised – she was born lacking that gene – or shed it at puberty. Her Visigoth prow – gives tongue. 'You needn't be looking for her here. She's with her Intended. Don't be bothering her at all, take my advice.' Turns her back. Door shut. I walk away. Walk on. The Hag. I'm glad to have met you. Again.

And, indeed, why should I complain? The narrative flows. The 'Intended' is intended to create dismay, fuel retreat. But she always has an Intended – the way she moves. I know no dismay. Retreat is not an option. I feel – and it's a charge – the town forming a wall. Instinctively, they're defending their December Bride, fighting for Granuaile, Jack Frost, Ernie O Malley, for they don't know what. The haunting fear that somewhere someone may be happy. I've stopped outside a cobbler's. Look at him in there, monkish above his last. Memory of a disturbed daughter, cobbler's, lifts from a spidery window of *fadó, fadó*. Dissolves. Rain commences. Only dry rain.

I make for Errislannan, four miles out, going south. Surprising how quick day is in December. Afternoon but the light already turning in on itself. Film of ache – *chronos, chronos*, but, contestingly, blithe alliance also with that light, shifty escalier palette of the coast, the solstice, the chase, haystack and roof-levellers of the obsessive, diva sway of her features, tutelage ineffable of her brown-blonde *trilse, na trilse ór-dhonna*, blown, thrown, tousled, hallowed, cinctured by whatever it is that cracks the pulse, decrees the cliff, no saving hand, *la scene à faire* …

A cottage. The cottage, hers. Easily found – what offers decliv-ity is. Bit of a gate – this blest timber knows, daily, her hands. Usual small rentable-off-season cottage, Connemara staple. Quiet. As your clay. Knock. Listen to the non-answer. Knock. Listen again. Walk a circuit of the place. Most windows curtained. You come to one that isn't. One that sings. A picture. Kitchen this could be. In the segment that's visible – curtain half-drawn – there's a chair. Scrubbed deal. December fingering it – orison. Across the back of the chair, a scarf I know well, angora, a certain enveloping purple, what purple is that, royal purple. I stand there, nose to the glass.

The drive back to town. It's raining darkness now. My state is tall excitement. The entrechat release of that scarf. A sighting, the first sighting. She's around, she's here. I'd – forgot to mention – caught her scent from the scarf. Summer lavender. I'm told there's such a thing as olfactory hallucination. No doubt – but that was not hallucination. I'm on track. One grief: that I'd been unable to reach in – it was no distance away – collect that trophy. I can feel silky texture of the angora on my fingertips. That hallucination? I've felt that silky ply sufficiently often to know that what is now on my skin is not hallucination. Is. Isn't. Is. All right. Nothing is but what is not. Axiomatic! In the attic. Where I – levitate. And be.

The town with its faerie lights. My plan is now so, so simple. Fundamentalist – I was brought up among warring sects, funda-mentalism my early anchor and helm of oak. My plan is to meet her. Here in this town. By searching until I find her. It shouldn't take long. It didn't take long – time did not enter. I met her over and over – in bar, hotel, supermarket, this street, that doorway – but each time close inspection denied me. A wet evening in the off-season tourist-trap looking into the illumined faces of young women. Nora Barnacles all. She has a Nora B complex – you won't be surprised to hear. 'We should live in Trieste for a while. Zurich. Kildare Street.' Her little games. I love her little games. But to find her inside the games. To find her. Anywhere.

The shift, at a heady bend of the evening, to asking people, whom I scarcely knew, if they had seen her around. (This was ab-negation, I know, I know, I must be delivered unto mine enemies.) Some refused to answer my question, some said, 'Pardon?' and passed on. One told me to go to the Garda Station. One suggest-ed I check the phone-directory. I'd thought of that, I'd remarked that the cottage had no phone, for example. But, for obvious rea-sons, I had put the phone approach boldly to one side. I didn't wish to speak to her by phone. I wished to meet her. Put out my hand. Touch her. Say – bone eyes melting – 'There you are, *a chroí*.' Enjoy the – startle – of her full regard. And. Ands seething ampersands.

Last card in my hand. It was getting late, while actually earlier, much, than many people thought. Her family place. Ten miles out. I'd been there often. In that kitchen, her father had said to me – 'Were you born near the sea?' She'd heard the question, heard my answer – only one answer to that question if in a blazure hour it's proffered. She could be out there. Or the sister – one of the sisters – would know where she might be found. But – ideally – I'd knock, step into the roomy solace of that kitchen – bowl of her making – offer greetings, take my seat beside her. Kingstown. 'The Kingstown people dressed in black / Pickin' winkles an' cartin' wrack.' Old late-night wine-on-the-table shanty of hers.

An enjoyable drive. The good dark, smoor of rain. A climb – that was good too. Illusion of the glass rising. No moon. I was there – in seconds. The house, low-slung farmhouse, in darkness – as, I suppose, I'd known it would be. Signs – to say the least – of occu-pation. A dog barked within, showed at the scullery window – col-lie, they always had a collie – defiantly pawed the door. I didn't get out of the car. It was enough to be there. Sitting in the car outside the house, hands on the wheel, a sound came to me. The shore. I could hear the shore.

'Listen to the sea,' somebody or other had counselled me on the splink of jook and duck and slobberdegullion mishap. I'd found it helpful – within limits. So I listen to the sea. Try to listen to the sea. Gable of the farmhouse. Maybe step out and lean against that gable. No, don't. Pull sustenance from it directly. A gable can be salvation, true. Perhaps. The collie barking. Where are you? We two. Same ten-mile radius – have been all day – and haven't met. You're so close. Must be. Collie quiet. Call of a curlew – that has to be the curlew. The gable again invites me, no, not yet. 'I will not be your veiled octoroon.' Listen. Don't listen. Do. Don't. Go on listen, go on, you're entitled. Listen. Hear them? Yes. Octoroons – unattached – stir in soft-pedal sounds of the sea.

Tusitala encore …

Not a pick on him. Hops up and down like a deranged heckler. Can't stop talking. But listens well. Wears pyjamas mostly, odd socks, one cocoa, one magenta. A deal of *moriturus te salutat* to him. Loves nature, loathes nature – 'I feel under attack from it all the time. I delve – lovingly –

'When Adam delved and Eve did span' –

'Who was then a gentleman?' I fondle the blade of grass, and, as I do, brume surrounds me, closes in. I don't mind. The life – the Pan life of plants – is Pan dead by the way?'

'Cod on slab.'

'Greatly missed. Plants – my fingertips could dibble forever, this is the contradiction – while I grimace – and wait for the horror to interrogate me. Horror of clay, creeping things, the void – no lack of void, no lack of void. I married a besom.'

He pulled up the magenta sock, watched it flop back to its preferred droop.

'Sometimes, Tusitala, I fancy you're a grasshopper.'

His kissing laugh – *lacrimae* in it too, *rerum*.

'Grasshoppers ahoy! You've sung the song, you call that singing –'

'You've sung the song, now dance the dance!'

'Met Hughes the other day. Wrote too much prose, he said, my immune system collapsed. Me? I settled on a precipice. What's your precipice pastime?'

'I peg shoes at her.'

'Does it work?'

'No.'

'Then what do you do?'

'Tell her stories.'

'Does she listen?'

'Sometimes.'

'Tell me one.'

'The two were happily married. Soberly moored in cove matrimonial. No children.'

'Always wish I'd fathered children.'

'One evening, six o'clock, they're sitting down to dinner, in walks a rat, clears her plate, clears his, strolls out.'

'I'll warrant you.'

'They didn't discuss it that evening, sometimes it's good not to discuss matters. Next evening, six o'clock, dinner on the table, the rat arrives, clears both plates. Again, they don't speak of it. If you don't speak of a thing, who knows, it may –'

'Un-happen?'

'That's it. Third day, the same sequence, and now they discussed it. The cat – awol – would be needed.'

'A story about cat-power – I knew it, by God, I knew it.'

'Shall I continue?'

'Story about claws, pussy, cunning little vixens – I damn well knew it.'

'Shall I?'

He fiddled with the cocoa sock. Nodded.

'They found the cat, discussed the matter with the cat, petted Her Ladyship, and she waited by the hearth. Six o'clock, the rat arrives, stickler for the punctual.'

'That's true, by the way. And little remarked.'

'The cat advances. There's a brief skirmish. The cat, frightened, retreats to a corner by the hob. The rat dines well, and departs. Silence in the kitchen.'

'Good – I like that – good.'

'After about half an hour, the cat slopes to the door, looks out carefully, checks the yard, and departs. And returns next day – about, say, noon.'

'The faunal hour!'

'Accompanied by the biggest cat you've ever seen, Tusitala – and you have wandered far – cat the size of a suck-calf. The couple looked after the cats.'

'This couple are learners!'

'The cats waited – a potent presence – that house buzzed.'

'Of the musky feline!'

'The rat arrived on the dot. The two cats advanced. They fought for three days in the kitchen, three days in the yard, and three days on the shore. At the end of the nine days, there was nothing left of the rat. The two cats tidied up – walked off arm-in-arm – and were never seen again.'

'Punishment? For inattention to the musky cellarage?'

'Has that smell, doesn't it?'

Tusitala, glum, considered. The story was not very much to his liking. At this moment, he looks rather as in the Sargent portrait – weirdo, pretty-boy, the big eyes, chalk (somehow or other) bones. 'Well,' he mutters to himself, 'maybe they deserved all they got.' I judge it wise to let the hare sit – alongside those cunning little vixens, percolating civet ... And I brace my hams for retaliation – he'll fight – it's not men that drain his colour.

'I see a grasshopper', he comes out with, 'perched on your left nipple-o.'

'Would it were a butterfly.'

'Or a moth. Don't put down the moth, Butterfly of the Night, they say. It seeks the flame, even unto burning of the wings. My besom springs diseases on us. Angina pectoris the latest. I ask the doctor, physical collapse? Close to, he says. Mental, I enquire? Don't rule it out, I'm told. The forest, and the sea, what else is there? My hand is a thing that was. I will go this far, my touch, I admit, is a mite uncertain in a love-story. Women, this whole woman problem, I'm no longer in fear of them, age makes the petticoat less opaque, don't you think? Never transparent, but, what I'm afraid of is grossness, do you take me? Not but I spent my youth in brothels with the best, was I awake? You know the bother with a love-story – I'll tell you – you have, it seems, to live it ...'

Tusitala into an hour-long spasm of coughing – I nurse him. During a five-minute gap in the middle, the subject of Father Damien, the Leper Priest, engages us – illnesses, excesses of, were on the table. 'Father Damien, met him, the man was a wonder, index finger invariably moist from some clit or other – that was part of his wonder, loved that man ...' *Momma mia* – lifelong adherent of the Loved Leper Priest – shrieks from her drumlin clay.

'That,' he lights a cigar, pours the Burgundy, 'was a most awful row with Henley but his rancorous attack on Fanny, she was ill again at the time, to make matters worse, that left the friendship beyond repair. My public disputation with Archer, the good William Archer, that was pleasantry, don't mind the coughing, my complaint is quite unknown, therefore, happily, will allow of no prognosis. Sound like Beckett? Archer – "That aggressive optimist, RLS!" I flung Thoreau at him – "What right have I to complain, who have not ceased to wonder?" That shut him up. Grasshopper's now on your right nipple, I notice.'

'You've sung the song –'

'You call that singing –'

'Tell us a story, Tusitala.'

'The forest – it's almost more alive than the sea. The one is the other, if you ask me. But the forest – pig, boar, serpent, eagles that know, tricoteuse trees, whoop of the gale, implacable downpour, never from heaven, that's another rain altogether. And spirits, abundance of spirits, take abundance from abundance –'

'Abundance remains –'

'The spirits, this is true in many parts of the world, I understand, certainly true wherever I've landed, you get to know them, y'know, partly, at their most dangerous they come in the guise of beautiful young men and women. Meet one of them, woe betide – you'll be charmed out of your wits – but – is that, of necessity, a bad thing?

Desideratum, some might say. I knew a man was sitting at home minding his own business. He'd cooked a fish – what more wholesome occupation. The man had cooked a fish. There's an concrete sentence, note the Saxonisms. I prefer the Gaelic – English, dear boy, has been abstracted to death. Two beautiful young women came down the road. That could be the start of my next posthumous novel. Dressed as God made them – sometimes (if in my glee) I give them kilts, pipes, sporrans containing ambergris, caviare, other dainties. *Civet!* Could they – if the man didn't mind awfully – have some of his fish? It was not in his nature to refuse. He shared the fish. And there was talk, they were conversable, fun and games, well-nigh, could have been a christening. Now, the man's not backward. He knows he's entitled to reciprocity. One of the beautiful young women is wearing a red necklace. Might he have it? Certainly, the woman – let's call her Red Necklace – said, I'll give it to you by and by. The two women then left – without ado. Vanished. As women will, their gift – among gifts innumerable. But they come back, sometimes, she came back, Red Necklace returned. Towards night, if they return, it'll be towards night, that's my experience, Auld Reekie to Samoa, he hears a woman crying that he should come now and she'll give him the necklace. He responds. He got up and left the house, followed the direction of her voice, *mulier cantat*, he followed, and his path took him to the edge of the forest, and there's the sea, that old collusion between river and sea, if I'd known that in time … Anyway, he stood on the *cladach*, you have that word too, stood there on the stones and looked out, there she was standing on the waves, calling to him, his heart opened to her. He wasn't up to it. Sank to his knees – the kirk weighed him down – sank to his knees and prayed. She disappeared. That moment did for him. They have to be followed – question doesn't brook argument – don't you agree?'

'Why must we follow them?'

'Because they know.'

'They've eggs that know –'

'Precisely, old chap, they've eggs that know.'

129

Bread in my hand, I took him out to a shed in the backyard. Turf galore lying there. 'Wait now,' I told him. A minute passed. Up out of the turf came a bird, thrush size, no feathers, the bird, instead, was clothed in ermine, shining white. More to come. Up out of the turf again, an ermine, that pure white angelic blaze against the turf, lamp for the needy, bar the speck of black, tip of the tail. Together, we gave bread to these – apparitions. Holy Communion in the backyard shed. Celebrants, we received, and were – momentarily – present, at one.

Opened a Book, a Page

Knuckles white, the father went about his daily bread, he'd tried to quell them but it was useless, the hands had a yen to clench, and, when hands clench, protuberant knuckles whitely shine, he must be a man, he deduced, whose knuckles enjoyed an independent streak, would take no counsel. He'd thought about the matter, left it there – he wasn't one disinclined to think, ask questions of himself, not, let it be said, spear questions, but with their own wishful integrity. He was always, for example, suspicious when he felt all right, such a state would be examined, the dictum *Never feel all right when you feel all right* had been vouchsafed him at some stage, and retained; he, allow it, suspected wellbeing, attitude, he estimated, that had stood to him over the dour haul – but, come the hour, proved protection insufficient – if there was anywhere available sufficient protection, and that he'd cause to doubt.

He'd never have forecast the nature of the assault, never. Without warning, plague descended: air-locks, ringings, cracked whistlings, drugged flutes, both ears, disorder the warrant. He said nothing to anyone. As recompense, a book opened, a page, a word. *Tinnitus* – 'A ringing or whistling in the ears, not resulting from external stimulus.' Quite. Therefore, internal. Physical? Forget physical, his instinct had already swept him past that consolation, he knew himself to be dealing with another climate, other shore. Did a map exist? This map. Misrule in the sound-box of his head belonged to the air, the ground, the night, was, as of this telling, neither malevolent nor benevolent, simply there, always, it would have you believe, had been, and, autocrat, had selected this moment to assemble the verities in whatever guise they might emerge.

Say nothing – wisdom there. Do something – wisdom seemed. Lough Derg, he decided, he hadn't been with years, Patrick's Purgatory, so hiked his trousers to the knee, and, barefoot, trod the gravel before the house in preparation for those bladed beds. This was necessity, the hardening of the soles – but it carried a disadvantage, made him the focus of attention, enough to trouble but not dissuade. From his first appearance on the tame practice-ground, the girl trailed him, absorbed in the reticle of blue veins which distinguished his feet – could she touch? – crayon them? – where'd they come from? – would they stay? – had they names? From an upstairs window, the boy took pretend photographs. The mother wrote her letters in the garden, prodded lightly. 'Took a notion, did you?' 'Call it that.' 'And, shure why not?' She quarter-smiled, knowing her man. He studied his knuckles, all present, buoyant.

After a week of the gravel, sight to see, he called off Lough Derg – there was general disappointment. Too bad. He'd had an intuition, possibly the first of his adult span, he preferred, as indicated, doing his sums, the ledger, but this jump – intuition was *jump*, physical in its intensity – he knew for gold, welcomed accordingly. Lough Derg, at the end of the day, was parade, thump-the-craw and pilgrim prance, leaving one side the unleavened bread, and tea so-called, closer to emetic. *Here*, right *here*, it came to him, was his seat of penance. Suffer it out on home turf. Hold. Listen. You'll be advised.

Momentary fee-fi-fum of the bold step. Rapidly then, the price to be paid. Pleasantries receded, had never been. A man on the street – with some gross satisfaction – remarked a harsh slope to his chops. The girl kept viewing him, sidelong, for confirmation of the truth, tinnitus gradually expanding the score, impudent, abrasive, assuredly she knew, she could hear moss travelling the stone. The mother, of a certainty, could measure the visitation, she'd a way of listening through the eyes, brand of hearing enhanced by sight, he'd married her for it, those clerical-grey eyes that had heard too many stories, his in the audit, and well before he'd met her. The boy, upstairs window boy, doubter-elect, knew, it was in his capacity for silence, those who know say nothing, Chinese proverb, those who don't shout. All knew.

Now a progression (retroactively biased). A hawk, plump sparrowhawk, bush-whacked him in the grounds one evening, and, whip of understanding, he could acknowledge Mistress Tinnitus no accident, meant, rather, blood bequest. Taking a dander to still the beating mind, he spotted the sparrowhawk in the act of ripping apart, consuming, some unidentifiable smaller bird that had life in it yet. His gorge heaved – 'They eat without bothering to kill' flashed through him. He would get out of there, rid himself of nausea, but – same time – he was gripped, caught in the deed. Sudden, it was too late. The hawk fixed him, yellow blaze in the stare, yapped – 'You should have been your brother,' – returned to the pulsing feast. He walked away, not about to look back, no, come to that, need.

And, in swithers and swives, considered. His ears were, sweet irony, clarified, douse of the incident had quenched the cacophony – but he wasn't misled, didn't rejoice, the remission, he'd wager, would be brief, there was a mountain ahead, pig-backed, must be met, climbed. Weariness clogged him, thicks of despair. They provoked, he was surprised to recognize, a kind of submission – that, in turn, earned response. He was standing by a Douglas fir, earthy and conversable the time flowing from its brimful trunk. Rest yourself against that tree, was his urge, rest a body. The tree made invitation. As he hesitated, bark melted from the trunk, peeled away givingly, and a fine auburn, desirous, beckoned – *Take ease here, close your eyes*. He obeyed, received that gift, skin to skin, on palm, on cheek. And heard a step. Steps. Not far away. His life, before this hour, moving back from him. Leaving.

J'accuse. 'You should have been your brother.' Several broth-ers in it but no contest. He could point, call. The one who died from sleeping in ditches while on the run. Jimmy, Jimmy *a ghrádh mo chroí.* Jimmy – on his path – had never been occupied by the trivial, was opulently clear in the messenger brow. *Credo.* A merry thing in his shoulders that had to do with lying down in the fire, unknown to anyone, sensed by everyone. Forged secret. Jimmy was on a list, head ringed in photographs. The Tans came to the mother and said, 'Ma'am, see the church tower below there? The day we shoot your son dead, we'll hammer the bell in that tower to spread the news deep and wide.' Jimmy. At rest, full military honours, in that very churchyard.

Tinnitus, as he'd anticipated, had effected a qualified depar-ture. A new orchestration, high-pitched hoodlum *kek-kek-kek* – friend sparrowhawk – moved in, *kek-kek-kek,* and a bony throt-tling around the clock. Still, he said nothing, felt alone, and sur-rounded. The girl wanted him barefoot, those high veins, want-ed to touch them – 'Them blue nets.' The boy watched from be-hind trees, whiff of spy to the child, undertaker – God save the mark – reconnaissance. 'Are you all right?' the mother asked. 'Never better.' 'Good.' And the quarter-smile. 'You went off Lough Derg?' He side-stepped the enquiry, wanted to give her his whole story, discover what it was, what that unburdening would do for him, them, for day, night, morning silences. While he deliberated, the chance flew past.

Move up a gear. Taylor the barber came one night, white coat starched and ivory buttons, ivory gills, confessed he was – as the town suspected – a British agent, adding, 'What harm?' Christ knows. He'd brought a sherry-glass containing some colourless liquid. Setting it on a table, he declared – 'The cup will tell you what you drink, don't worry your head about that,' – and left, whistling a George Formby song, tune to the song, familiar to all, it spoke of 'leaning on a lamp-post at the corner of the street –' and – 'o, me, o, my, I hope that little lady comes by …' A British agent. Great pity the Brits could never learn to stay at home, sing

'Drink to me only', polish their ramrods, stump their overs. The drink sat there, nothing would persuade him to touch it. After two or three hours, he took a slug, and found his mouth, tongue in particular, festooned with slivers of glass. Fear stiffened him to a plank. Nor could he cry for help. It was the girl who came, fingers agile and informed, removed the slivers one by one.

That was dawn, Sunday. Jimmy came to him during second mass, there in the Sanctuary, Jimmy bright in the brow. The bells were sounding for the Elevation of the Host. 'Talk to the bird,' said Jimmy, 'bird'll give you a lot more nor the time of day.' The visit wasn't unexpected, he'd felt the approach of it over several days, threshold fuss, but now, in no hurry to open negotiations, delivered himself to a flurry of bowing, breast-beating, counted white knuckles, none missing, lifted his head. Jimmy beside him, slim, gentle, a witness. 'Talk to the bird.' 'You talk for me, will you?' Shower clattered against the stained windows. Father Maguire's surloin neck. The stooped congregation. 'You talk for me, Jimmy.' Jimmy, leaning close, played an understanding finger along misery lips of the accused.

A bargain, let us hope and pray. The father endured. Months later, among barking spectators at a football match, the hawk landed on his shoulder, wiped its beak on the overcoat, Sunday best, just been dry-cleaned. And he was elsewhere, schoolboy self, listening from shadow to men talking in the byre, talking about Dermody along the mountain who had wife and daughter living on tin clippings, every penny going to a house down the road where there was drink and a Biddy in charge who'd do the men, do them if there was a score in it, no bother, do them again before morning. The wife and daughter laced Dermody's tea, dragged him out to the pigsty, pulled off his britches. They had the best knife in the house handy, and, from gelders visiting, knew the way, nothing to it, left the patient there to discover himself in his altered state, went back to the kitchen, tidied up. Basin o' water. Towel. Throw a few sods on the fire.

The Feeding Ear

Girl missing, the boy travelled the grounds. Not a trace, and the spaces conspiratorially still, as though she was in seclusion, and the trees, bushes, long grass, frilled moss and layers of beech-mast all banding to assist. Roaming an alley, he called after her – *Merci beaucoup … Whipster … Ye whipster, ye … Dominus vobiscum … Bad cess to ye!* … He stopped by an elm, weakness in him often for the broomstick noggin of the elm, witch skelter of it. But the noble fir was – most of the time – his standing weakness, that misted disdain, modesty of it. Not forgetting the sycamore. In the wise toddler phase, they'd found (and at ninety-three would again) him under a sycamore holding a Kerry cow by the tail, world suspended from the turning filament of noon. A crow cackled. *Girl missing.* He moved on, yodelled, sang 'South of the Border' in his Gene Autry twang, and, when he came to *mañana*, held on to the word, made of it reveille – *Mañana … Mañana … Man-nyannnn-naaaaaa …*

Girl asleep, body set against some louring weather … One hand a red fist, other open, showing the nails bitten, never seen biting the nails but they didn't bite themselves was the house verdict: chastised, she'd look at them as if they belonged to an impenitent Eskimo … Breathing easy. Small mouth puckered but, as everyone said, lucky with the lips, full lips, rare in the lipless world of the hills …

The mother-beech. He climbed into it, girl could be there or the grandmother might be able to advise. Grandmother not to be seen but he could touch her presence, she wasn't far off. He went to inspect the idol, since he was in the vicinity. It had less shape to it, face slurring back into the timber, features uncertain, bark dull, unfriendly. He laid his hand on the lump of it, heard the grandmother, she was trailing him all right, gurgling above, cistern, chest, reservoir, and a gush, waterfall, the perfumed flood, crashed through branches beside him. She arrived, settling her skirts. 'They made a hole in your head?' He nodded. 'Nothing wrong with a hole in the head,' she pointed, and there – miss it if you didn't have the know – was the hole in her forehead, slightly left of centre. 'Have a look.' He put his eye to it, saw the girl, in sunlight, she put out a tongue at him. The grandmother, amiable, pushed him away. 'Some quarters that's how they say hello, flap o' the tongue.' 'Show me again, will you?'

Your sister sleeps. He could study all day the girl in repose … That hair now, page-boy cut, moved between blacks and browns, depending on the day, the season. No smidgin of curl – but it worked, played, talked of quiet, open doors, surprised pool. It was his custom to check the hair of girls he knew, hair was power – he'd seen the sparks, the flame, hair was magic, was – it made windfall sense – thoughts, thoughts flowing, the story was, must be, in ripple of the hair. None he'd catalogued so far – bar one, possibly – could match the girl's for filigree. Stretching, he took up a strand of the sleeping mop, it lilted between his fingers like spring-water …

'Show me, won't you?' She wouldn't but she would 'dispatch him to travel'. That was code for hypnosis, long promised. 'Do.' 'Are ye fit?' She murmured into his closed eyes, wrapped him in care, he gave assent, went away, landed on the quick-way to school, autumn morning, the spiderweb world, there wasn't a breath but for the weave of well-being, he was walking in health, everything was fresh from the well and true, all the more true because, built into the scene, live in the selvage, was guarantee of the temporal, this is forever, therefore short-lived, understand, love now the gossamer, goose-summer, *clábar*, the Michaelmas pot, gander's hiss, goose-egg in the hand, ochre and lemon the ditch – he was back from it, grandmother swiping gossamer from his shoulders, tucking it around his ears – 'Feed the feeding ear, *a mhic-ó!*'

'Go into graveyards much?' She knew well he did. 'Fair bit.' 'Dangerous paddocks for some.' And she told him about Jemmy Cullen. 'Was working in Raffoney Graveyard with a few of the brainy boys, putting a shape on it, s'posed to be, maybe they were. Didn't they plant a stone in a spot where, sound chance, Jemmy's spade'd meet it, falsified stone, *Jemmy Cullen, RIP,* carved on it, and above that, for badness, a Bishop's Cross. Jemmy's spade, sure enough, walked him to the stone – the gougers made themselves busy in dip and hollow, gave him room to inspect it. When they had a gawk, he was going down the lane, spade left behind, there it was propped against the stone, it's there yet, they say. Straight with him to the bed. Held on the three days. Burial yesterday.' 'Jemmy's gone?' 'Correct!'

Door of the room where the girl lay sleeping, boy watching, swung open. The calico Tom entered, reconnoitred, advanced, jumped onto the boy's knee, and – adopting, smoothly, the boy's line of vision – examined the girl. This for half a minute. The cat shifted, sprang onto the bed, stalked to the foot of it, looked again at the girl – who hadn't stirred. Cat taking in the girl, cat features the mask. The girl whimpered. Cat, standing position, listened, right to the tip of his tail, awaited further transmissions. The boy slept, met with a windgall, slurpeen of rainbow, hung in the southern sky, you could eat it. He awoke. 'Sign of storm,' the cat advised. 'What?' 'Windgall.' He yawned meditatively. Final neutral inspection of the sleeping girl, the Tom jumped off the bed, departed, tail beating the silence …

Rest in peace, Jemmy. No white foal for the girl. Near pigeons, far crows. A thrush. He saw that spotted breast, took it inside him, half-a-mouthful in the hand, heard the sound, no sound, of the father treading gravel, a permanence. 'I should keep far from graveyards?' 'Stay out of them and go into them.' More of her ould guff. Nettles, she lesson'd, made by far the best soup. This had to do with Eve in the Garden, Ould Slitherer in wait and coiled, daylong, under a nettle-tree. 'That soup's one ripe brew.' Mention of the Slitherer shook him, she caught the tremble. 'Slitherer's not the worst. The bite's a kiss if you're up for it.' She let that strangeness sit for half-an-hour, finally came out with – 'A mighty number.'

She was dreaming now, eyelids active, giving off punctuation. She sneezed, sat up, and – from toils of her sleep – threw off the bedclothes. Nightdress fickle about her, she walked to the window. It was known she had the walking custom but he'd never seen it on display. She stood by the window, waver of green her background. 'When the pony died, the grass grew,' she said in an even voice. 'Your pony?' he asked, wishing he'd be granted the coup of talking to someone in sleep, to her in sleep. She didn't respond, simply brushed her fingers against the glass, turned, came back to the bed, into it, blankets up around her, resumed her favourite position, that curved suspense that was crowded always.

Leaving the tree, he glimpsed the mother, the father, the priest and the priest's dog outside the house, in puppety movement, going inside, coming back out, one towards the garden, another off down the back avenue, dog prancing and yelping, and, you'd be entitled to say, directing the whole confusion. He got out of the grounds without being noticed, headed for the demesne. The grandmother had given him a second go at the spy-hole. He'd seen the girl again, in timber, women around her, women of the cottages, a drove, had to be the demesne. The town first. Side-streets, measly and dozing, waiting for the factory-siren, that'd be soon enough. Oweny Lynch, ex-postman, home from The Big House, torn uniform back on, Turk of a man with a tiny face, stood confronting his own closed door, now and then set his nose against the knocker's spickspan. The Excel Cinema advertised *The Mark of Zorro* – not to be missed. And, out of a lane beside the cinema, now coming towards him, Jemmy Cullen, astride the Black Nelly, you could see through Jemmy, walls, windows, doors the other side of the street invading that narrow frame no longer flesh. Struck, the boy drew back, waved. From the departed – creak-creak of the wind-broken bike, the head down, fixed for good and all – answer none.

She slept. He enjoyed her looks. High cheekbones, strong chin, not red-cheeked like the country crowd but not pale either. She'd been pale, primrose, and she'd be pale again, but lately there was the tint of a glow, was that from the 'grandmother dipping' – as he'd named it – dipping of the girl's head in the foliage bath? There's the grandmother to the life, no guessing the next move, twenty jokers in the pack. And, foliage bath, the sound that went with that dipping, juicy-wafery antiphon of the beech leaves stirred by the girl, gentlest din, percussion and not. Put it to music. The pipes. Flute. Finger your stops and start the flow. Finger her cheek, he'd an itch to do it but fearful of bringing her out of the nap. Try it, why don't you? He ran a fingertip against the cheek available. She didn't stir. World of her mortal skin. You. There. And – your tenor – somewhere else entirely. Sleeping girl sighed. It was said that cost a drop of blood, went with the sigh. Cost him more than a drop to count it. Count the road inside it, furls it came from, miles yet to be, he winced to measure that sigh. Was he imagining its proportions – or tasting salt truth? Both. He was there beside her, listener, to imagine its propor- tions, thereafter taste salt truth. That sigh rose – and travelled with – and mingled with – the word fontanelle, the tune fontanelle, fontanelle open and closed but open the day at issue, dunt taken, that sufficient, didn't matter was the story true or not, it was true in the sigh.

At the edge of the town, dusk coming on, he met the women, a khaki straggle, the young, middle-aged, old, bowed under bundles of wood, seasoned branches they had leave to drag away, no charge except to body and soul, dragging that cargo a couple of miles, old rope or blue binder-twine around it, bunched fists making a stay below tight face, hard breath. Trail- ing them was the girl, bit of a stick in her hand, minding the flock. Procession hauling itself forward and past him, the boy fell into step as she came abreast. 'Took a ramble,' she gave him, brimming, regal, ragamuffin. The women left the road, turned up the boreen to the cottages, muster of shabby dwellings look- ing down on the Workhouse, the lake, The Plantin'. He and the girl stood there, observed those loads, uneasy compact, on dumb backs of the carriers, little to be seen but brown blotch of the loads this final stretch of the haul, silent ascent that owned the rise, arraigned it, slow vanishing then into backyard or shed like drawings erased, bruises, a memory.

Rick-Ma-Tick of It

It was decided she must go to school, Girls' National, that was the next step, September came round and droves going back to school or commencing and why should she be left out, she had her entitlements, and, who's to be judge, the school shenanigans might be exactly what was wanted, drag her out of herself, the company would be good for her, regularity, better nor counting daisies, shouting at bumblebees, and Sissy Sands, teacher-in-waiting, knew the form, as, surely, did the other teachers, and the children, for that matter, Sixth Class down to High Infants and Low, they, too, would take her in stride, so, it's arranged, this fine September morning she sets out, new leather schoolbag, shiny purple, strapped to her shoulders, pencil stowed, pencil-parer, ruler, jotter, bottle of milk and sangwedge, hand in the mother's hand, composed face of the mother leading the way, short walk down the hill to school, children flowing out of the sky, gabble and screech disturbing the crows, the girl curious, incautious, waving to everyone, waving to herself, delighted, up and down like the tinker's new apprentice, teacher-in-waiting Sissy petted her sad bun, again tacitly resolved to do her best, please the Lord, not her first time round this steeplechase, incidence high in the hills, cross-breeding or the clay ('Fit only for mules with the head-staggers,' her man said) or something in the winters or black visitation, just, and pitch them, poor things, a year in school was the woeful practice, a name in a roll-book, it satisfied something or other or it satisfied nothing, nobody knows and nobody cares what the King of the Monkeys wears, scrunched wee *rawnee*, the mother handed her over, cheek a peck, and departed, the girl's formal education had begun.

And it was bees' knees, cat's pejimminies, there was drawing, slates, chalk, all colours, it was playing, that's what it was, she found friends who were friends already, sortov, more the faithful minders, Marsie Ryan and Bernadette Kelly, they minded her here, were on her side, and when a row ruz over a pencil straying, hair-pulling or nail-scratching or name-calling – some tramps from the cottages weren't above calling the girl 'an imbisill' – they were quick to intervene, drive back the little crabs, dry tears, restore colour, she'd turn sheet-white at mention of that *imbisill*, mightn't know the word but she got the lash all right, Singing Class was the best, *Doh ray mi* up the hairy mountain and down the feathery glen and *Beidh aonach amárach*, the words were slippery, hard to hold on to, but the girl, it was noticed, was quick to the tune, hear it, she had it – or most of it, she, more than anyone else in High Infants or Low, *opened* to the singing – that went, Sissy had cause to believe, with something missing, sod gone from the load, music, the singing, was permitted to fill the gap, she'd met it many's the time, but this one was, God bless her, exceptional in that regard, she'd lift off the seat, hammer time on the desk-lid, let the words – bits of them anyway, but the bits *ablaze* – whirl inside her, she'd spin, grow wings, beatification ring on her forehead, rest of them were fozy turf, by comparison, scraw, 'You're a credit,' Sissy'd say to her, whisper mostly, look out into the yard in case she'd spill a tear, school nothing but singing this hairpin'd be belle of the ball, break your heart if it wasn't already in peesheens. Aye.

Anyway, whether or which. She settled in, all things considered, fairly well, couldn't be stopped fiddling with the abacus – 'A harp it is,' she told anyone who'd listen, twangling the wires and sliding the beads about, pretending to count them, playactor and *glic* enough, she'd nearly convince you she was counting, before taking off into strangely unkempt laughter which entertained – vastly – the gang around her, and, indeed, Sissy, at first, but Sissy, like the rest of us, had her warp days, and, one scourge of a migraine Monday, deemed herself compelled to enquire before the lot of them, matter-of-fact as you like, why the laugh, if it wasn't an impudent question, and couldn't it, come to that, be done without or confined to outside of school-hours, the girl's eyes whisked, and, in lieu of answer, or for answer, she nod-nodded, divil's own nod, pen screeds on it if you'd no more to be at, it seemed to be saying *Yes* to everything, the most cooperative *Yes*, keen to oblige in every way, that kind of *Yes*, while, in fact, in school, class, lesson fact, it was the original verifiable donkey's-heels-dug-in non-starter, sabotage and villainous, wispeen grin about her jib tossed in, Sissy choked hard, went and wrote on the blackboard – 'Nobody knows and nobody cares / What the King of the Monkeys wears …' gave the pack of them ten minutes to learn it off. 'What's it mean, plee'Miss?' Stella Ward asks from the top of High Infants. 'What it says.'

Leak in the roof, you don't blame the rain, do you? Say nothing, and maybe it'll wash a window, propagate the cabbages. But had Sissy known the tantrums she might have discouraged the parents – then would they have listened to a word she said? Child supplied the regular – one a week, on average – mother-and-father of all tantrums, poison your craw if you didn't know to steady your gaze on the dry-rot floorboards, Sissy's palliative, High and Low Infants needed no refuge, devoured every last thrash and tumble of the fit, couldn't get half enough, circus peepshow, no charge, the girl would – no warning, no evident reason – transmogrify to a soldered little knot, shaking, howling, eyes shut, ears, fists, entire zoo shuttered – bar the gob howling, spasms of this to a berserk gazebo, it could last five minutes if she was in top form, next stop Transylmania, that the place, bats with teeth, the cure – until the next outbreak – rested in the ministrations of Marsie and Bernadette, they'd bide their time, spot a comma, children *were* a mystery, slide in, soother and collogue, horse-whisperers in the name o' God, animal-trainers with secrets passed down, they'd stroke and hug, inch her back from wherever she was to living daylight, by inspired touches undo the knot, find a way through rear-up and gone-again, free the unfortunate from her revulsions (buried 'ithin), three-minute job, five at the most, behold her now, Her Ladyship back from the front, smiling cartwheels, perfectly 'normal', perk to her gob and pinafore-so-blue, *Dominus vobiscum* and *Merci beaucoup*!

Being who she was, she had her opposite of the tantrum, depend on it, unnerving in its changeling way but nowhere near as unnerving, she'd sail off into herself for a good hour, sit there in a daze or a doze while the world went on without her, lost but contented lost, you'd be willing to say, and you wouldn't on any account interrupt, she might break like a saucer, no, let her lift from it in her own time, and she would, refreshed, ready for anything, like the day she landed back from travels of that description, raised her periscope to find Watson watching her, spotted her straight off, Watson, the Inspector, *an Cigire*, overqualified weasel in his Harris tweeds and the Ballymena *smig*, not a word to spare for a dog, leftover (and knew it) from 'God Save the King' time, and, by the by, had a bit of a stutter himself, the girl stands up, makes for the visitor with her bag – by special permission – of sweets, stops fornenst him – 'Take one, won't ye, there's lots' – the clem didn't know what to do, looked at her, measuring her, speechless, stutter forms but trips on a diphthong, and the girl, sipping *an Cigire* through dewy perplex of the certified innocent, enquires of Sissy – 'Is he, is he a Prodestant – or what?' *Slán leat*: Watson, lip hanging a side of bacon, doesn't reappear for a twelvemonth, *from the mouths of babes*, they were right proud of her that day.

One thing you could draw consolation from – and it was wanted – the children (most of them) perfected a way of *in*cluding her while admitting that – being what she was and who – she was *ex*cluded, pattern, yes, but always remarkable, children had elastic in their eyeballs, lose it soon enough, they had it now and they'd yield it, give them full marks, but *they* didn't have to control a class and her in it, nothing'd pay ye, there should be homes, institutions, something for her like, school was *school*, you kept coming back to it, and for those *meant* for schooling, Little Miss wasn't of that persuasion, she'd ejjimikate herself, let that road take her to heights of scholarship unknown or lump her marooned where she was, gawkeye, airing that cuckoo laugh and strumming an abacus into grey hairs, ask the King of the Monkeys' pink backside, Sissy one spring day, asked her – girl, by this time, sidelined, secured, better, in Low Infants, unemployable extra, Sissy asked, wondering why she hadn't long since, 'What's going on in that nignoggin of yours, *a chrot*? The girl, to general astonishment, came back – 'Why did the hen cross the road?' When the roolye-boolye had diminished, Sissy suggested – 'You tell us, why don't you?' – and the star-turn loosed her nod-nod, laughed (that laugh), and, chalk handy, busied herself courting the letters X and Y, her two favourite inscriptions from the broad slopes of learning, Sissy, patience wearing, and small blame, as spring ambled towards summer, conceived a plan of teaching her the letter Z, part for the sake of completion, part vent for exhaustion, but it was useless, she'd no time for that letter Z, wouldn't, she declared, 'touch it with a forty-foot pole', spake she'd collected from Heck Cassidy, the postman, during the Easter holidays, and enjoyed the stretch of, Sissy let it go, it'd soon be summer, the creature had lasted the year, they'd all lasted, no harm done, the last day she ran off with the rest, came back with the present of a double-daisy and to collar 'her' abacus, then away with her playing her harpstrung banjo, and crooning '*Beidh aonach amárach*', ask Sissy for her final verdict, she'd say in that tired and tireless croak of hers, 'Tell the truth, I saw far worse, she'll go her own way, leave tracks too, but you'll never find her, won't be there, always somewhere else, God bless her.' Pause. And she'd add, 'I done me best anyways.'

For I Stand by the Gate Alone

The mother took a silver christening-cup from the sideboard, sat down at the table, tin of Brasso and cloth handy. Silver. She had her doubts. Silver in it. The real thing wouldn't so easily tarnish. She studied once more what was written on the cup, job to make head or tail of it on account of the over-ripe lettering, froth of curves and curlicues, leave you light in the head – *Presented by Supt Joe Murphy & Mrs Murphy to mark the birth of Marie Celine, Jan. 18th, 1935*. Superintendent Joe. Pompous little man and odious eejit, latest announcement he intended leaving his dress-uniform to the nation. National Museum? Or local – specially erected for the bequest. Roadside shrine? And what of the corpse, hadn't he thought of mummifaction or – *fiction*, which was it, in the old high Pharaonic mode? Freezing? No, attentive, as he was, to the seductions of posthumous strutting, he'd skip those temptations, go, discreetly, untreated, but, like the saints and martyrs, survive incorruptible, be discovered so, by adherents hell-bent on fomenting a cult, and so extend his ever-extending fame and glory. St Joseph of Magheraroarty. *Pray for Us.*

A rabble of scrubbers, as Father Maguire was wont to put it, had rogued into the Force when it was being founded, Flying Column Joe among them, fired one shot in the War of Independence (it grazed a superannuated ewe, a law case resulted) and gained officer status because his wife was a distant relative of the Blacksmith of Ballinalee. Joe should have been an actor, hamactor – or, closer to it, a clown. No Musical Society, no Social

Evening, was safe from his depredations, but, Ireland being Ireland, times being the times that were, it was in the line of duty his popinjay leanings thrived – the gadabout climate favoured the combination of clown and Guardian of the Peace. Example: it fell on him, as might have been prophesied, and probably was, to arrest General O Duffy, the Monaghan Mussolini, that time of the big meeting in Westport, Joe skipping onto the platform as O Duffy began to rant, Joe, with Browning drawn, armed plain-clothesmen and photographers at heel – 'General O Duffy, I arrest you in the name of *Saorstát Éireann*. You will, I can assure you, be treated as befits your rank.' Switching the revolver to his left hand, he saluted O Duffy, cried out – 'God Save Ireland,' and, cheers for the General, vituperation for warrior Joe, the Blueshirts were left to supple their night-sticks in pubs by the quays.

The cup. The christening-cup. A curiosity about it that had, from day one, niggled. Simple thing. Look for your reflection in the silver (which it wasn't) and, this, she knew, had to do with the curve of it, some law of physics, your face always came up elongated and screwbald. That apparition, her own distorted face, had frightened her the first time, still disturbed, something in it, beside it, that gnawed. This was, fine, irrational. But also rational. The one because you couldn't engage in a battle with the laws of physics, the other because we all have, and are entitled to, a healthy desire to see our faces plain. Part of the bother was that she was compelled to seek for her reflection in the cup's surface on a regular basis – unable to put it aside. The circumstances. Clearly. The cup marked a given. Was a given to mark a given. She, the house, all of them, could have done without the cup – post-factum, certainly, but, also, at the time. For why? The donor, what else. And therefore it made incomparable sense, above and beyond laws of physics, those discovered and those still to be, that, when she sought her reflection in the cup, a grotesque mask looked back at her, clown Joe somewhere inside it, purblind and accusatory.

She spilled Brasso on to the cloth, and – thinking of nothing – applied it vigorously to the outside of the cup. The inside, much tarnished, colour of bogwater a sunny day, she'd given up on long since. The cup wasn't a day in the house, and the inside had that bloom of tarnish. She blamed it on the champagne. Showman Joe had brought a magnum of champagne, and insisted they all drink in turn from the cup. Something in the champagne, she was convinced, had acted on the metal, the amalgam, silver and whatever else was in it. And something in the champagne (she never took champagne) had given her a headache for ten days. 'To the First Girl,' Joe had toasted, smiling his foot-lit, spot-lit, and buck-teeth stage-smile above the dozing child. And went on to recite the poem he'd written for the occasion, tinsel verse which, happily, had gone missing, wasn't mourned, now presumed lost, forever, Amen.

Ball the cloth to leave a dry section available. Patiently, she polished. The surface brightened, took on lustre. Maybe it was silver. Maybe – just to see his eyeballs stutter – she'd ask him – 'Joe, is that, if you don't mind my asking, *real* silver?' What got to her most about Joe – and it had taken her a while to concede this – was that he was, apparently, *un homme fatal*. Much talk of *la femme fatale* but what about *un homme fatal*? Meaning not quite the same thing, allowance made for gender, not quite the same – but worse, probably, if you cared to examine it, and she did, the phrase fascinated her. *Un homme fatal*, as she understood the matter, was destined for disaster, and, accordingly, created a disaster-zone around him, mourn for those in close proximity. Joe's credentials in this respect were impressive. The wife, poor-mouth Pauline, eighteen months ago, sudden mortal illness – cancer, you could see it coming, *hear* the life draining out of her. Teenage daughter, a ghost on wheels, never born. Male child, cot death, few years back. Of Joe himself it was known that, when stationed in Burtonport, he'd twice driven into the sea (clear summer nights, full moon), and survived, the lakes hereabouts, he'd jest, had their eyes on him, he might, tho', just might, discover them less amenable.

Who are you? She inserted her face, twisty, in the shine. Who might you be, Madam, when you're at home and the door locked? How dare you – fiddlechops – interrogate me, none of you damn business. That's grand, if you've no wish to talk – but it might have been a useful conversation. Useful? Beneficial. In what way? All kinds of ways but mostly within ways. Within ways – worse ways, I suppose, than within ways – yes, go on, go on. Thank you, well, here's a question – one you won't hear on *Question Time*, Sunday night at eight, the programme for happy families that are all alike: what do you believe in – or, repair the final preposition, in what do you believe? *My salad days, when I was green in judgment.* Piquant – you're obviously a purveyor of pert ironies, that's the glitter – near-glitter – in the restraint of your eyes. *Pert* is the only term I'd quarrel with there – I'm well past *pert*. Delete *pert* – leave a blank, and hurry on, so many miles to babble on, what do you regret not doing? Don't brood on it – that invites duplicity. I regret, perhaps, not going into the garden, Maud, on hearing that invitation, and, on being assured that the black bat, night, had flown. You got that invitation? O, yes. And received those crucial assurances? O, yes. May we have the vibracious details? No. You're quite sure about that? No. Meaning No to the vibracious details or *No, I'm not sure*? Ever hear – *Time Jesum transeuntem et non revertentem* – pardon my French. Translate, please. Fear saviours passing and not returning. Tell us more. He was impossible – in the loose sense – and flowers in his hair, that's all, next topic. Thank you – and, not to push my luck, you have, no doubt, other – lesser – regrets, which might be of interest to our listeners to this edition of *Question Time*, the programme et cetera? Sorry, what was the question? Regrets, other, lesser. *You see me, Lord Bassanio, where I stand.* And where's that? Why, sitting at this table, a christening-cup, tarnished, gift of a fool, in my right hand. Thank you, and – is there anything you'd like to add – I only make the suggestion because you're so clearly in the vein – some little thing – luminosity – or, say, some